Volume 1
2020

Welcome to the premiere volume of *Numb*, a collection of short stories, flash fiction, poetry, short screenplays, sketches, and art. Did I leave anything out?

I am a firm believer that art is life and life is art. So, what does that mean? To me, it means that the act of creating—in whatever form you choose (writing, art, music, design, etc.)—is an essential aspect of life. I would have a very difficult time going through my day-to-day life if I didn't produce something. I've been this way since I was a young boy—always drawing, writing, creating fantastic stories in the wonderous worlds of my imagination. As I grew older, I took classes on creative writing, painting, and ultimately screenwriting and filmmaking. I simply love to create.

The second part of that phrase is that life is art. We can choose to live a life filled with beauty and creativity; a life that is designed and tailored to produce aesthetic attraction and emotional elation. This can be as simple as filling your home with furniture that is designed for visual appreciation as well as comfort. Or filling a room with floral arrangements and objects that provide a visual aesthetic and produce joy when you enter. A life of art is taking the time to make a meal a presentation on the plate, not just placing the food there without a care. A life of art is a life of intention to create a visual, auditory, olfactory, and tactile environment around you.

The publication you hold in your hands is one element in this lifelong journey. I have attempted to create an experience that is artistic on multiple levels.

There is only one rule in *Numb*: there are no rules.

I am a firm believer that there are no rules in the act of creation. Just look at the platypus … But seriously, the cover of this issue is a prime example. There are designers who will scream: "You can't use more than three fonts in a design! This is wrong." To which I would respond, "Tell that to Storm Thorgerson, Filippo Tommaso Marinetti, and the editors of numerous counterculture publications." I grant you this, you can tell me you don't like my art, but you can't tell me it is wrong.

I hope you enjoy this issue and the issues to come. Most of all, I hope you live an artful life.

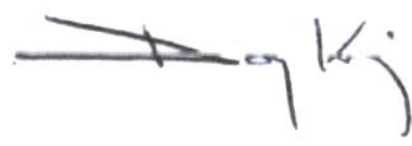

CONTENTS

THE TYPOGR

Short Story

Poetry

(poetry by Douglas King unless noted)

Typographical Art

APATHY ISSUE

PRINTED IN THE UNITED STATES

NUMB is a curated assemblage of new writing, photography and art, providing a platform for creative talents to showcase their work.

Published by:
Day III Productions, Inc.
dayiiiprod.com

Publisher:
Douglas King

Copy Editor:
Jessica Manley

Original photography sourced from Unsplash.com.

WE WANT YOU

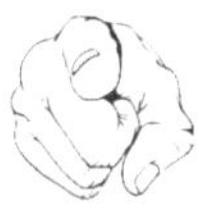

TO SUBMIT YOUR WORK

If you are a writer, screenwriter, illustrator, artist, or creative in any way, we would love to see your work for consideration for publication in a future issue of NUMB.

Please submit your writing or portfolio to:
Doug@dayiiiprod.com

Wake Up

Words: Douglas King

Original photography
BK - @woolyart
Unsplash

Wake up.

The soft female voice was stereotypically angelic.

Wake up.

Thomas heard the voice again in the darkness of his mind. He mentally reeled as the vestiges of warped dream images faded and the realization that he had fallen asleep to the rhythmic rolling of the train car rushed to his consciousness. He cracked one eye open and saw just what he was expecting: the gentle smile of Mac—short for Mackenzie—and he immediately wished she was his girlfriend, not just the person with whom he currently shared a first-class passenger car on the way to Inverness in Scotland, or simply an acquaintance he knew through a mutual friend.

"What were you dreaming?" Mac asked.

Thomas rubbed his dry eyes.

"Eh?"

"You were mumbling in your sleep. You had to have been dreaming," she said, smiling.

Thomas focused on her face and drank in the flawless, fairy-like features as if he was a dehydrated man drinking from a desert oasis.

"So why did you wake me?" He responded, a bit more curtly than he wanted.

"Sorry, Mr. Grumpy Pants." Mac folded her arms across her chest and sulked—staring out the window and biting her lower lip.

Thomas was immediately convicted. "No, I'm sorry," he said. "I'm just not fully awake yet. Forgive me?"

He knew she would, and she did. Mac was too generous, kind, good-hearted, and all the other positive attributes to pout or hold a grudge for longer than 15 seconds. She had once nearly made it to 20 seconds, Thomas noted, but then who keeps track of someone that closely?

Mac turned back to him with a bright light in her eyes and equal wattage in her smile. "So, tell me, what did you dream?"

Thomas loved (did he dare use that word?) how everything was a happy adventure for Mac. He often thought she would have made a perfect Care

Bear character—probably with a rainbow on her tummy. She was so childlike in her views on life. The complete opposite of how he felt most of the time. He wished he could share her rosy perspective, but a life of hard knocks and unrequited feelings had hardened Thomas and cast a pall over his attitude.

"Um, let me think." Thomas rubbed his palms over his eyes in an attempt to shut out the real world and capture his dream before it slipped into the murkiness of memory. "Okay," Thomas said and opened his eyes.

Mac was sitting with knees up to her chest, smiling, waiting to hear his tale.

"I was riding a beast of some sort—swaying back and forth. It must have been my subconscious compensating for the rocking of the train."

"Don't editorialize, Tom," she interrupted. "Just tell me where you went."

Thomas had to smile now. Mac was just too cute. She loved adventure in any form, whether real or imagined.

"So, I was on this beast. Big majestic creature with horns gilded with decorative gold sheathes encrusted with gems that sparkled in the sunlight!"

Thomas was good at telling a tale, and Mac was even better at listening. It didn't matter if every word was an actual description of his dream, what mattered was the passion with which he told it and the worlds in which they could travel together through his words.

"I rode in a basket on top of its back, swaying to the motion of each step," Thomas continued. "Next to me was a lovely woman. Her features were like those of a fine porcelain doll. Flawless. Beautiful."

Thomas knew he was describing the young woman sitting across from him, yet he hoped she was not aware of the comparison.

"We were traveling to a distant land to seek adventure and see an old friend. It had been a long journey but not an arduous one, and we were both enjoying each other's company and the scenery." Thomas paused to gauge Mac's reaction to his story so far and, like most men, was completely unable to discern any idea of what she might be thinking. *Why are women so cryptic*? Thomas wondered.

"Go on," Mac said, breaking Thomas' brief rabbit trail of thought.

"The two were falling in love …"

"You mean, you and the woman?"

"What?"

"You started the dream by saying 'I.' But you switched to third person," Mac said.

"Did I? You know how dreams are. One minute it's you in the dream, then you are detached, then you are someone else. Dreams are weird that way," Thomas said. He debated about how much of his dream he should really share, which was obviously his brain dealing with the fact that he was on a trip with a woman he had deep feelings for but could never—would never—express in reality.

"Anyway, he … I took her hand in mine. It was the first time we had ever touched intimately, and I was afraid I might be rejected, but she squeezed my hand back and I knew. I just knew." Thomas trailed off, lost in the vivid memory of that dream moment.

Mac sat quietly, enraptured by the simple tale, waiting for Thomas to continue.

"It was perfect. We didn't say a thing to each other. We didn't have to. You know how in dreams you just know what the other is thinking? It was like that."

"No editorializing."

"Right. Next, we were no longer on the beast. You know …" Thomas stopped himself before explaining dream logic, or illogic as the case may be, and he noticed that Mac had a slight frown from the new interruption.

"We were walking now. It was a skinny path through fields of grass greener than anything I have ever seen before. It was so lush and full of life. Blue skies, green grass, white pillow clouds drifting in the sky. It was like an Impressionist painting."

Thomas looked out the window of the train as a similar scene passed before his very eyes, as if he had returned to his dream. Or was simply recounting what was happening to him.

"I was so happy. We were so happy. Even though the woman and I had never talked about being in a relationship, it was like we just knew it was right. Like we simply knew we were meant for each other," Thomas continued.

He paused and looked into Mac's eyes and wondered what she was thinking, if she knew he was talking about the two of them. She looked back at him with her innocent, friendly manner. If she knew what he was alluding to, there was no registration on her face. At least none that Thomas could discern.

"We walked on like that, then I think I did start to say something. That must be when I was mumbling," Thomas said and caught Mac's frown again at his new editorialization of this dream. He quickly continued so as not to frustrate and lose his audience of one.

"I don't remember exactly what I said, but I think it was something like, 'This is such a perfect day. I don't want it to ever end.'"

"And what did the woman say? How did she respond?" Mac inquired.

Thomas thought. He couldn't remember the woman ever speaking in his dream, and he debated whether to lie and manipulate the story or simply state the facts. Suddenly, he felt flush and even a bit sick to his stomach, as if he now stood on the precipice of life, at least his love life, and the slightest move could send him crashing down into the abyss of loneliness below; a place he felt like he had spent most of his adult life.

In what felt like minutes, but in reality was only seconds, Thomas imagined a number of conceivable possibilities to how this dream, and the situation before him now, might play out. Like a chess player running through options, Thomas debated what the correct thing to say was, how honest to be, how vulnerable to be.

He decided to roll the dice, gambling that his story of two destined lovers might have found purchase in the heart of the woman he knew he loved.

"I don't know. That's the moment you woke me up. What do you think she said?" Thomas asked.

He waited. The two sat in silence. Again, time seemed fluid, and Thomas knew that the eternity he was living was only a brief moment for Mac. He waited, hoping her answer would wake him from the deep sleep his emotions had been lost in.

Mac looked at Thomas. Her eyes were like pools of the clearest water in the world, he thought. He waited, teetering on the edge of happiness or doom.

Finally, she said, "It would be grand if love happened so easily in real life."

Thomas knew it wasn't a direct response to his question but an answer true enough. "Yes, it would," he replied. "It would be a dream come true."

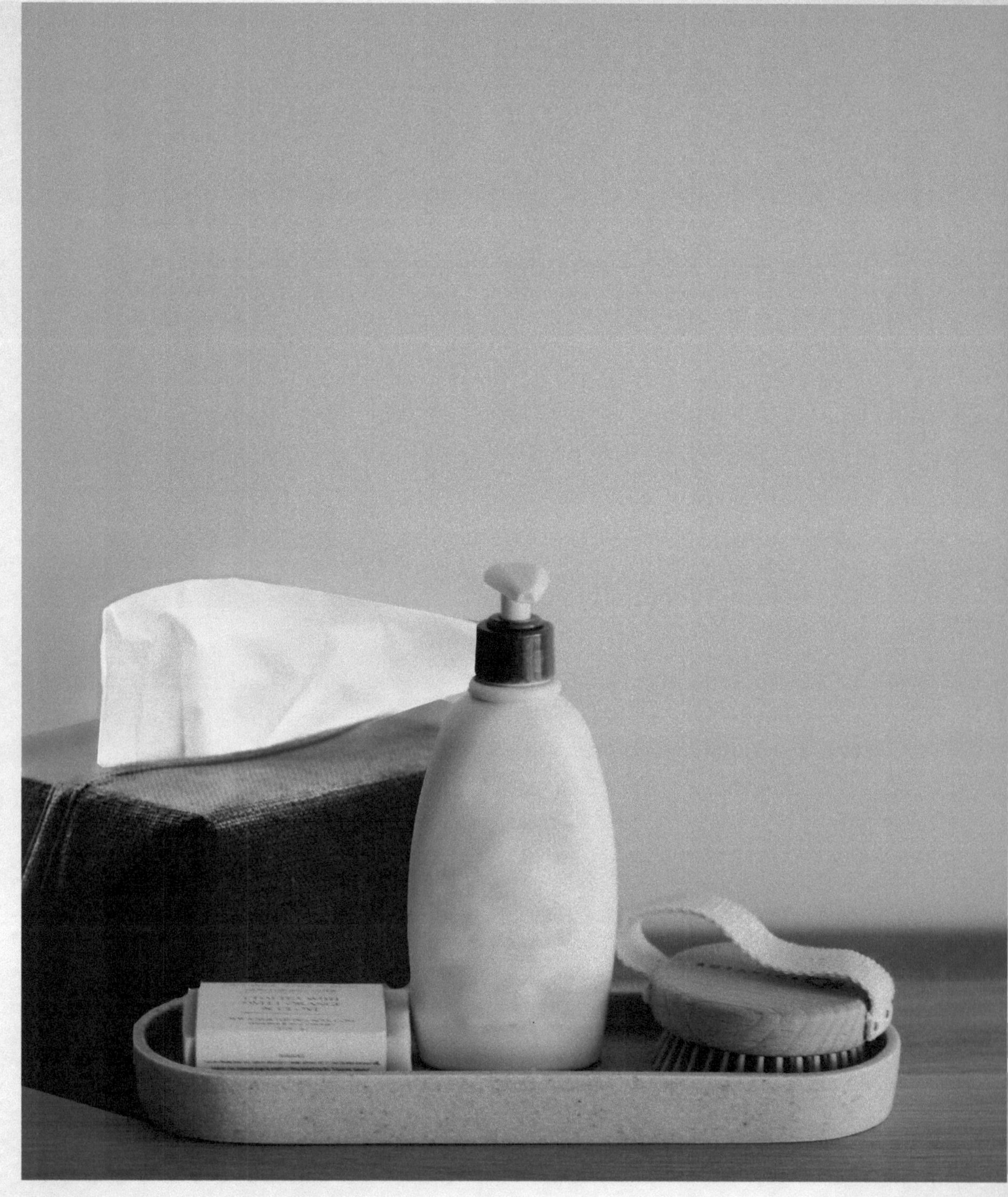

Instead of smelling like sex,
he smelled like cheap lotion and despair.

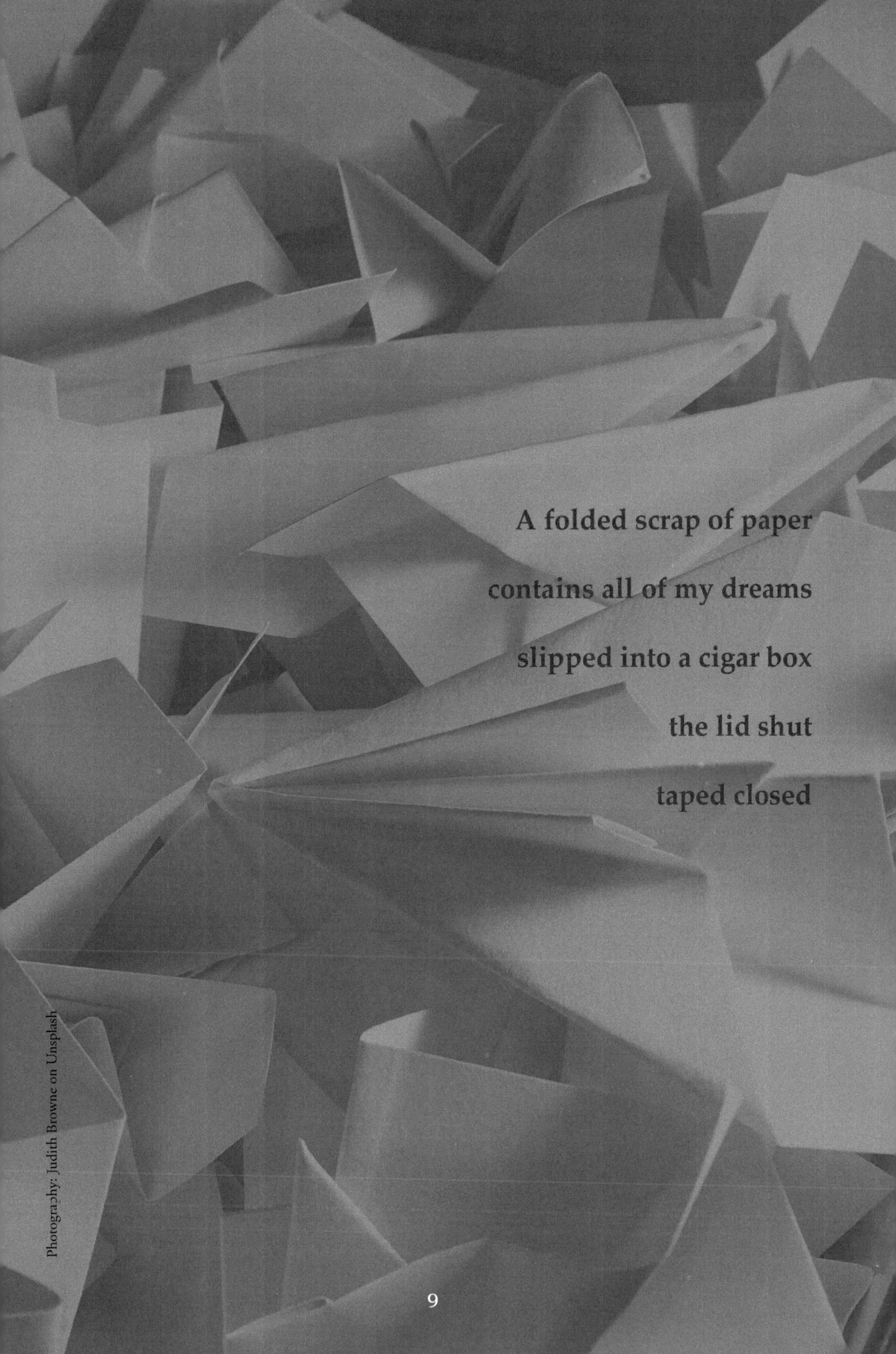

A folded scrap of paper
contains all of my dreams
slipped into a cigar box
the lid shut
taped closed

Photography: Judith Browne on Unsplash

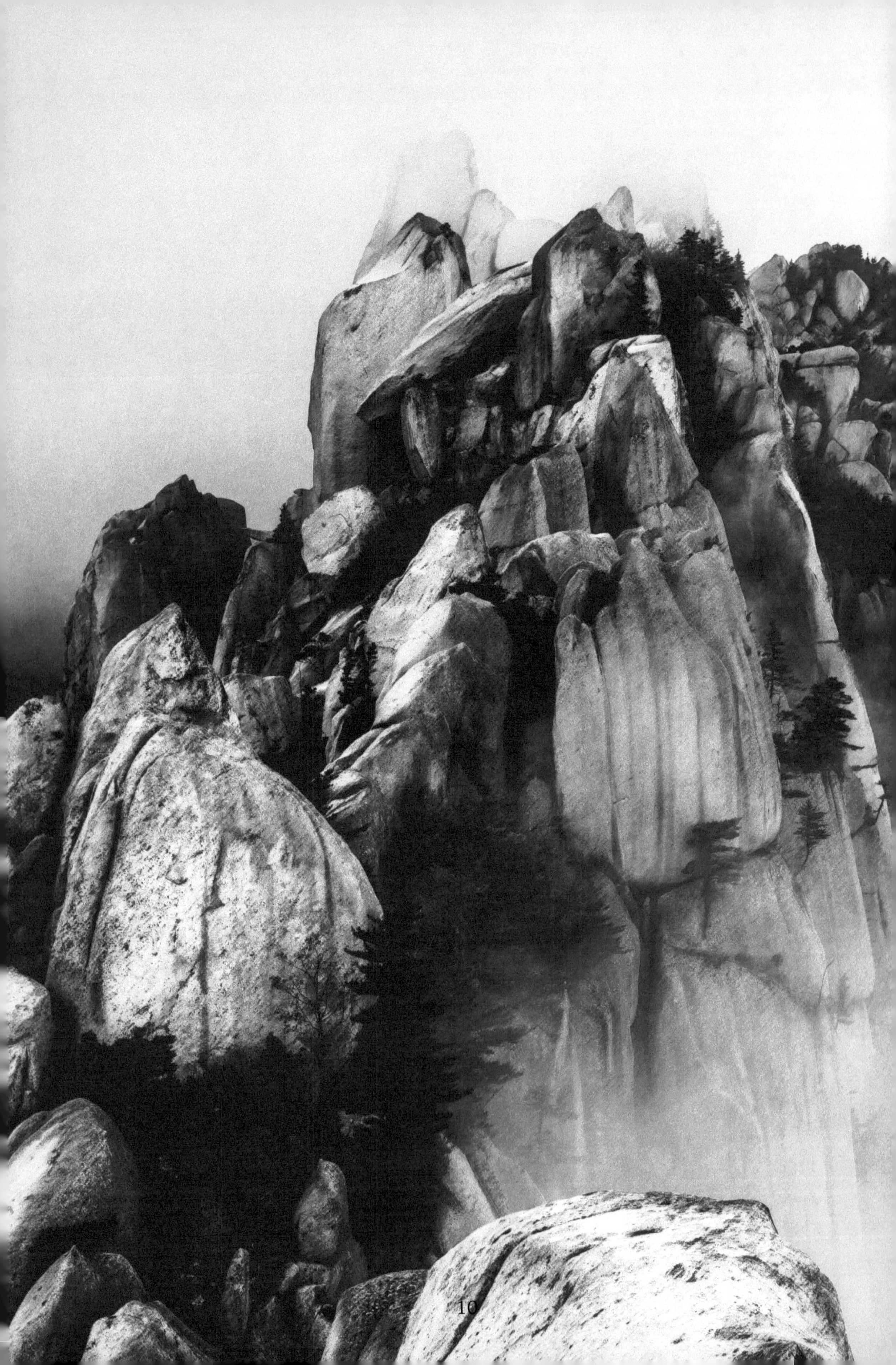

Hush
listen
the dew and mist
blanket us
in a fine coat

Silence
only broken
by the whisper
of saturated vapor
descending

Rest
knowing
all is well, all is calm
you only have to listen
hush

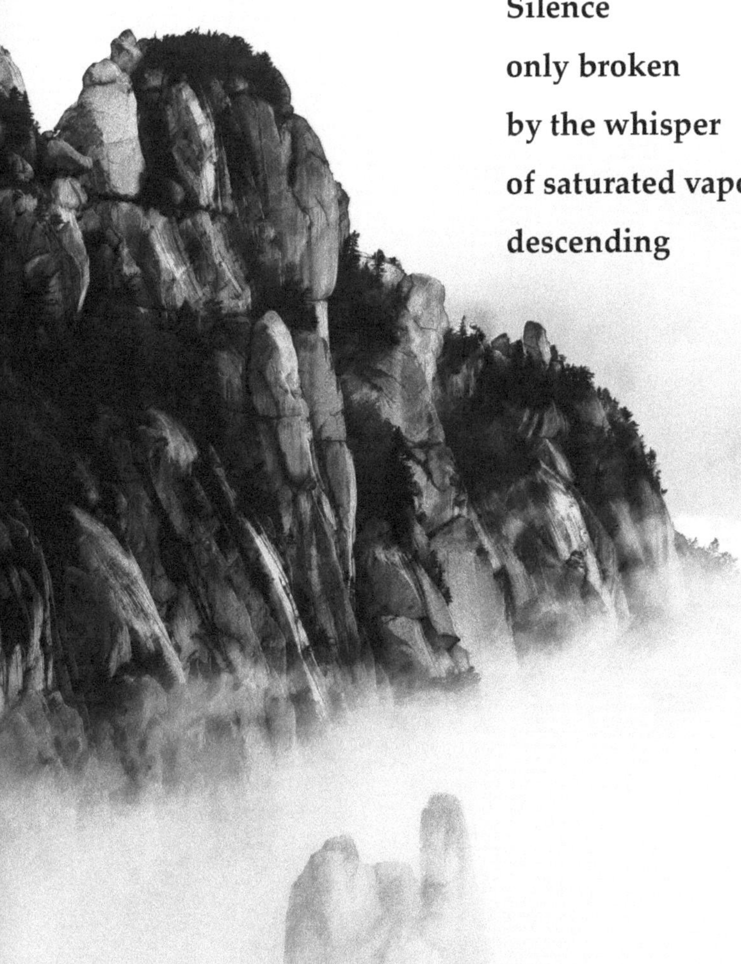

Photography: Alexandre Chambon on Unsplash

My happiest moments are just before FALLING asleep

My saddest moments are just as I WAKE

LITTLE MONKEY BOY

Written by

Douglas King

TITLE CARD - "MONKEY BOY"

SFX: Screaming monkeys are interrupted by the sound of screeching tires and a car crash.

INT. HOSPITAL WAITING ROOM - EVENING

NOAH HENSLEY (10) stares into the distance with a thousand-yard stare like a man twice his age who just survived D-Day. Dark circles outline his sad eyes.

DOCTOR (O.C.)
I'm very sorry. We did everything we could but your husband's injuries were far too severe.

JULIE HENSLEY (O.C.)
What am I supposed to do now?

DOCTOR (O.C.)
Be with your son. Comfort each other. We have a fine staff of grief counselors that I highly recommend you utilize.

INT. HENSLEY HOME - KITCHEN - DAY

Noah, HOOTING, throws food against a wall and swings his arms wildly. He bounces on his seat like an ape.

JULIE HENSLEY
Noah! Stop that!

Noah HOOTS louder and slams a bowl on the table repeatedly.

JULIE HENSLEY (CONT'D)
Noah! This won't bring him back. Stop acting this way! Nothing is going to bring your father back.

Noah calms. He hangs his head. He jumps down from the seat and, walking like an ape, leaves the room.

JULIE watches after him, concerned but exhausted. She surveys the mess he made and she now has to clean.

INT. HENSLEY HOME - NOAH'S BEDROOM - LATER

Noah squats on his bed. He grunts and pushes his toys with his knuckles.

The door opens and Julie enters.

JULIE HENSLEY
Hey, kiddo. You must be starving. I saved some food for you -- what you didn't throw against the wall. You want to come down and try eating?

Noah turns away to face the wall.

Julie crosses and sits on the edge of the bed near Noah. She reaches for him and strokes his head.

JULIE HENSLEY (CONT'D)
I'm sorry I yelled. I know you're hurting. I miss him too.

Noah turns and stares at his mother.

JULIE HENSLEY (CONT'D)
Let's get some food in you.

Julie tries to tickle Noah. He GIGGLES.

When she stops, Noah picks at her hair as if picking lice from her scalp. He puts his fingers to his mouth as if eating.

JULIE HENSLEY (CONT'D)
I meant real food. I doubt I have enough mites to give you a meal. At least I hope not.

INT. GROCERY STORE - DAY

Julie and Noah enter the store. Julie grabs a cart while Noah, arms wagging above his head, ape-walks into the produce section -- heading straight for the bananas.

JULIE HENSLEY
Oh, please not in public.

Seeing the bananas, Noah reacts excitedly. He hoots at the top of his lungs and grabs a bunch, clutching them to his chest.

A SHOPPER watches with disdain as Noah hops up and down HOOTING with joy and swinging a second bunch of bananas around in the air.

He is creating quite a disturbance.

Julie rushes to Noah and grabs the bananas from him. She places one bunch in the cart and puts the second back.

Noah screams and grabs the second bunch of bananas.

JULIE HENSLEY (CONT'D)
Noah. This is not how we behave in public.

Noah tosses the bananas into the cart and reaches for another bunch.

JULIE HENSLEY (CONT'D)
No! Noah. Put those down.

It is a standoff. Noah holds the bananas. Julie points for him to put them back.

The Shopper and now a TEENAGE EMPLOYEE watch with anticipation.

JULIE HENSLEY (CONT'D)
Put those back.

Noah hesitates, then throws the bananas into the cart.

JULIE HENSLEY (CONT'D)
Noah!

Noah screams, grabs another bunch of bananas, and runs off into the store.

Embarrassed, Julie returns one bunch of bananas to the stand. She glances at the Shopper and the Employee.

A HOOT comes from somewhere in the store.

Julie rushes off to see what trouble her son has created now.

EMPLOYEE
That kid sure loves bananas.

FOOD AISLES

Julie frantically searches each aisle looking for Noah. HOOTS come from somewhere. But where?

FROZEN FOOD AISLE

Noah stands in front of the ice cream section. He stares intently at the various offerings.

Julie finds him. Flustered, she pushes the cart toward him and grabs his arm.

JULIE HENSLEY
We are not doing this today. Here.

Noah SCREAMS like he is scared and hurt. He tries to pull away.

More SHOPPERS are watching.

Noah points to the ice cream. Julie follows his finger.

JULIE HENSLEY (CONT'D)
Monkeys don't eat ice cream.

Noah HOOTS and bounces. He continues to point.

JULIE HENSLEY (CONT'D)
You think they have freezers in the jungle? A monkey wouldn't have any idea what to do with ice cream. It would probably freak them out it is so cold.

Noah ponders this information.

Julie kneels down to be eye to eye with her son.

JULIE HENSLEY (CONT'D)
Listen. We can't make a scene in this store. Mommy has to come here ... a lot. So, you behave like a good ... monkey, and maybe I will teach you about ice cream.

Noah stares at her.

JULIE HENSLEY (CONT'D)
That sound like a fair deal?

Noah nods affirmative.

INT. HENSLEY HOME - FAMILY ROOM - DAY

ROBERT HENSLEY holds Noah's arms, and Noah flips head over heels with his father's help. The two LAUGH as they play.

Noah swings a number of times in a row.

ROBERT HENSLEY
That's enough, son. You've got to be dizzy by now.

NOAH HENSLEY
No. Can we do some more, please?

ROBERT HENSLEY
If you throw up, your mom is going to blame me.

NOAH HENSLEY
I won't. I promise. Just a few more.

ROBERT HENSLEY
You truly are my little monkey boy. Okay, here we go. Ready?

NOAH HENSLEY
Yes!

Noah takes his father's hands and performs somersaults.

Julie watches from the kitchen. She smiles as the home is filled with LAUGHTER AND MONKEY HOOTS.

JULIE HENSLEY
I'll make you both some termites on a log if you want.

NOAH HENSLEY
All right!

INT. MEDICAL OFFICE - DAY

The colorfully painted room is child friendly with affable clouds decorating the wall and a plentiful supply of toys in bins.

Noah sits on the floor moving blocks around.

Julie sits with DOCTOR CARTER. They watch Noah intensely.

DOCTOR CARTER
Noah never behaved like a monkey before?

JULIE HENSLEY
Only when he and his father played together. But never anything like this. He doesn't talk. He lashes out ...

DOCTOR CARTER
And this behavior began ... after the accident?

JULIE HENSLEY
Yes.

The two watch Noah as he tries biting a wood block, then tosses it away angrily when he realizes it isn't food.

DOCTOR CARTER
Well, it's obviously a coping mechanism. Noah is trying to hold on to his father, and one way to do that is by staying a monkey. He essentially has become a little monkey boy.

JULIE HENSLEY
Can you help him?

DOCTOR CARTER
I will try.

INT. HENSLEY HOME - FAMILY ROOM - NIGHT

Julie receives a NOTIFICATION on her phone of a incoming text.

She looks at her phone. The CALLER ID reads Dr. Carter. She opens the text to find a link to an article and a brief messages.

She reads her phone.

INT. HENSLEY HOME - KITCHEN - MORNING

Noah monkey-walks into the kitchen and leaps onto a chair. He HOOTS and bangs his fists on the table.

Julie turns to him and smiles tenderly.

Noah, bangs his fists on the table again.

Julie HOOTS.

Noah stops and stares at his mother.

Julie HOOTS again and then monkey-walks over to where he sits.

She cuddles Noah in her arms and begins to groom him with her hands, miming that she is picking lice from his scalp.

Noah sits silently. Julie COOS and makes random guttural noises that are soft and comforting, all while continuing to groom and cuddle her son.

Noah leans into his mother's arms and chest and cries.

TITLE CARD - TWO DAYS LATER

SFX: Children laughing and playing.

EXT. SCHOOL PLAYGROUND - DAY

Noah swings from the monkey bars on the school playground at recess. He is alone. He HOOTS and SCREECHES while around him other kids SCREAM and LAUGH.

NATHAN (10) looks at Noah curiously. Nathan approaches.

NATHAN
Hey, Noah, a bunch of us are getting a soccer game going. You in?

Noah stares at Nathan. Nathan stares back.

NOAH HENSLEY
Can I be goalie?

NATHAN
Sure. Who better than the kid who jumps around like a monkey. No one will get anything past you.

NOAH HENSLEY
Cool.

Noah swings down off of the bars and joins Nathan as they walk toward the soccer field.

FADE TO BLACK.

EVERYTHING IS Art.

Live a DESIGNED life,

But always remember,

None of it MATTERS.

Photography: Judith Browne on Unsplash

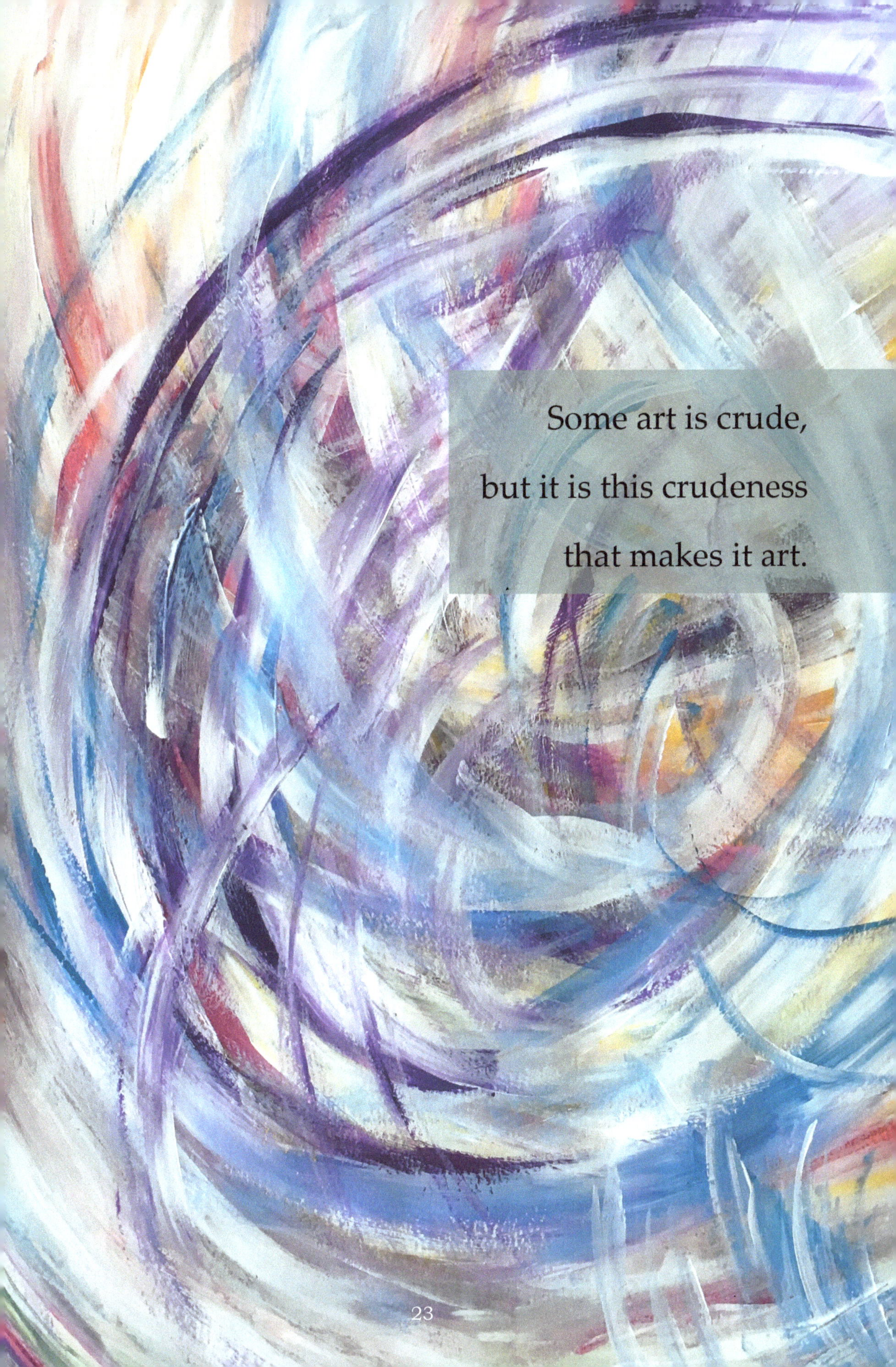

Some art is crude,
but it is this crudeness
that makes it art.

Annie Griffeth

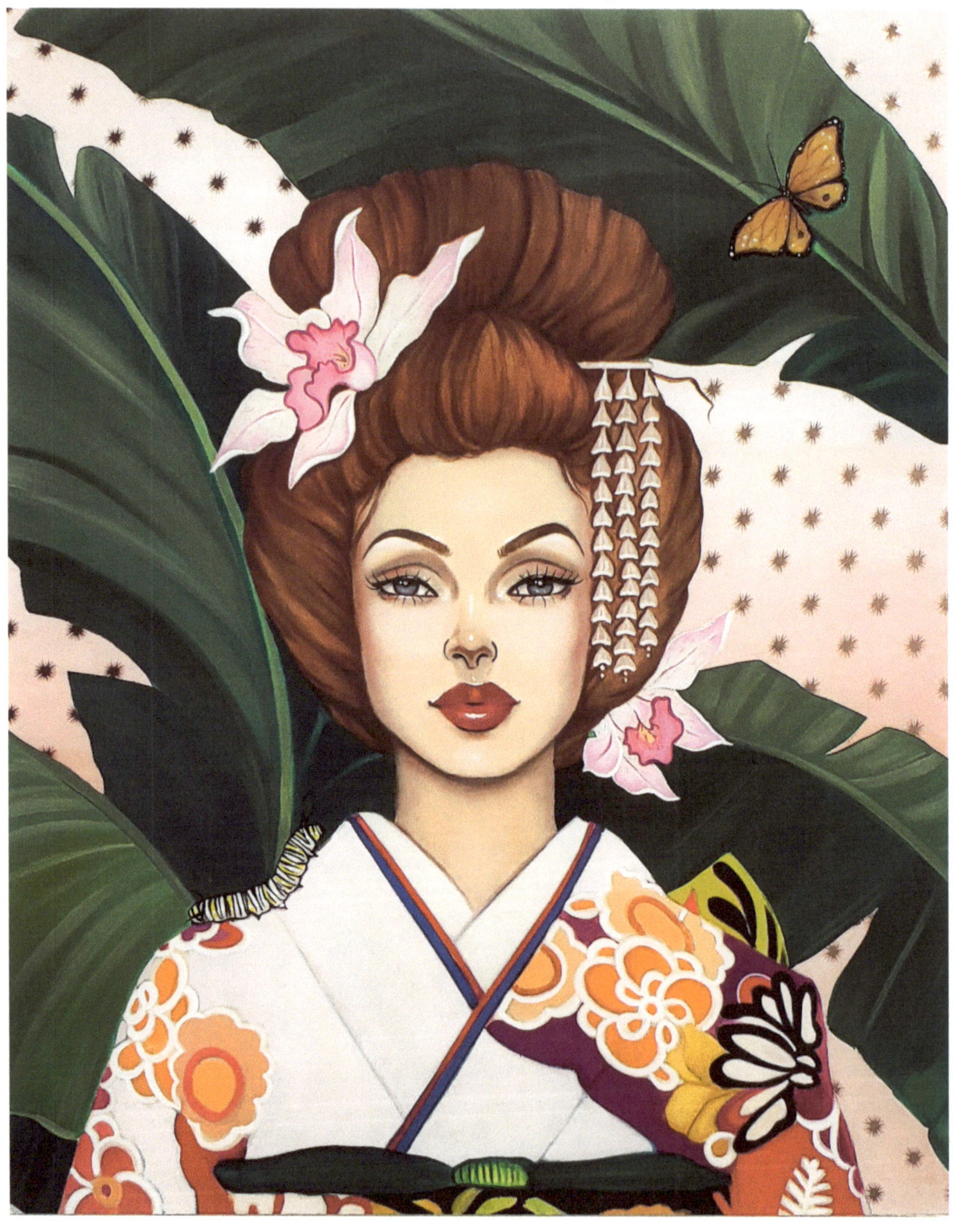

When you first meet Annie Griffeth you immediately notice something, it's that joy can be personified. Originally hailing from the North Shore of O'ahu, Griffeth is a multi-faceted artist who infuses magical realism with a Hawaiian and Asian aesthetic. Magical realism may be the best way to describe Griffeth, or at least what it's like having a conversation with her. She has enough energy for four people and her speech is peppered with witty comments, dry humor, and just the right amount of snark.

This attitude carries over into her playful artistic style and the work which is allegorical and employs symbolism to speak on social issues, transformative life events, as well as everyday joys and challenges. She creates ink drawings as well as acrylic and oil paintings on paper, canvas, and wood.

Griffeth is one of the four founding members of the ALG Collective, a multi-artist studio and showroom located in the heart of the Design District in Dallas, Texas.

ARTIST STATEMENT
My work is a conversation about things that give our lives purpose. No matter how different we are, we all share experiences that make us feel vulnerable or fierce, that give us strength or cause us pain, and are the reason why we are who we are today. I use symbols, colors, and words to communicate my thoughts, and if you find yourself understanding, relating to, or just "getting it," then we've both found a friend.

How do you define art? What is art to you?
Art is purposeful creation. In its highest form, it is the engine that moves society forward.

What surprises have you discovered about yourself, or your art, in the process of creating?
I didn't realize how important symbols would become in my work. There are symbols that are universally understood, across language and culture, which shows how powerful an image can be. A symbol that reminds you of someone you love or something you aspire to can change your mood, give you strength or resolve, and brighten your day. I think it's a worthwhile cause to bring more of that into the world.

Why do you create art? What is the main driving force to create?
To make art, you have to have confidence; to share it, you have to have courage; and if people don't respond the way you'd like, no matter how that makes you feel, you have to find the strength to go on. When I started this journey, my dad had just passed away unexpectedly, and I was so lost and in a great deal pain. But that pain became power by discovering these qualities within myself, through my work. Being able to express my deepest feelings healed me and changed me forever. Now I can't stop.

anniegriffeth.com
Instagram: @anniegriffeth
algcollective.com

previous: *Becoming*
20 x 24 in
acrylic, ink, and paper on wood

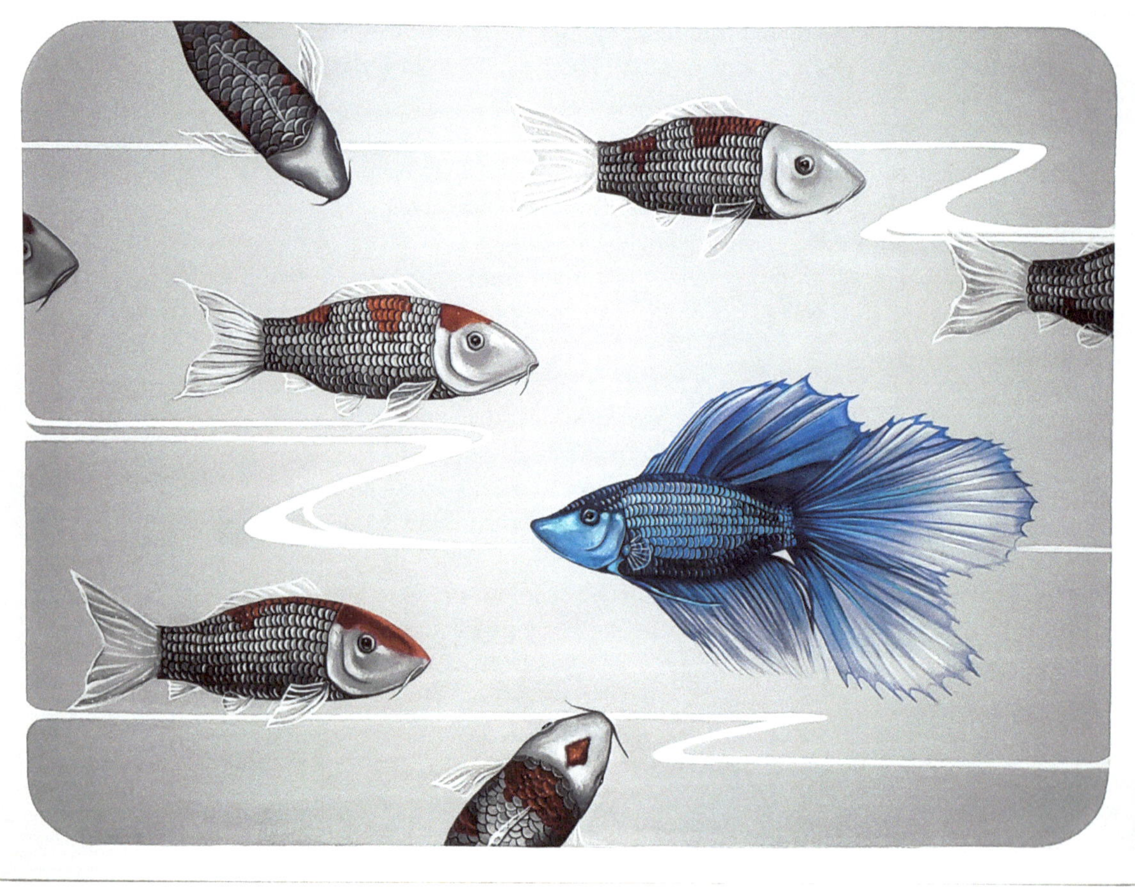

Against the Grain
36 x 48 in.
acrylic on canvas

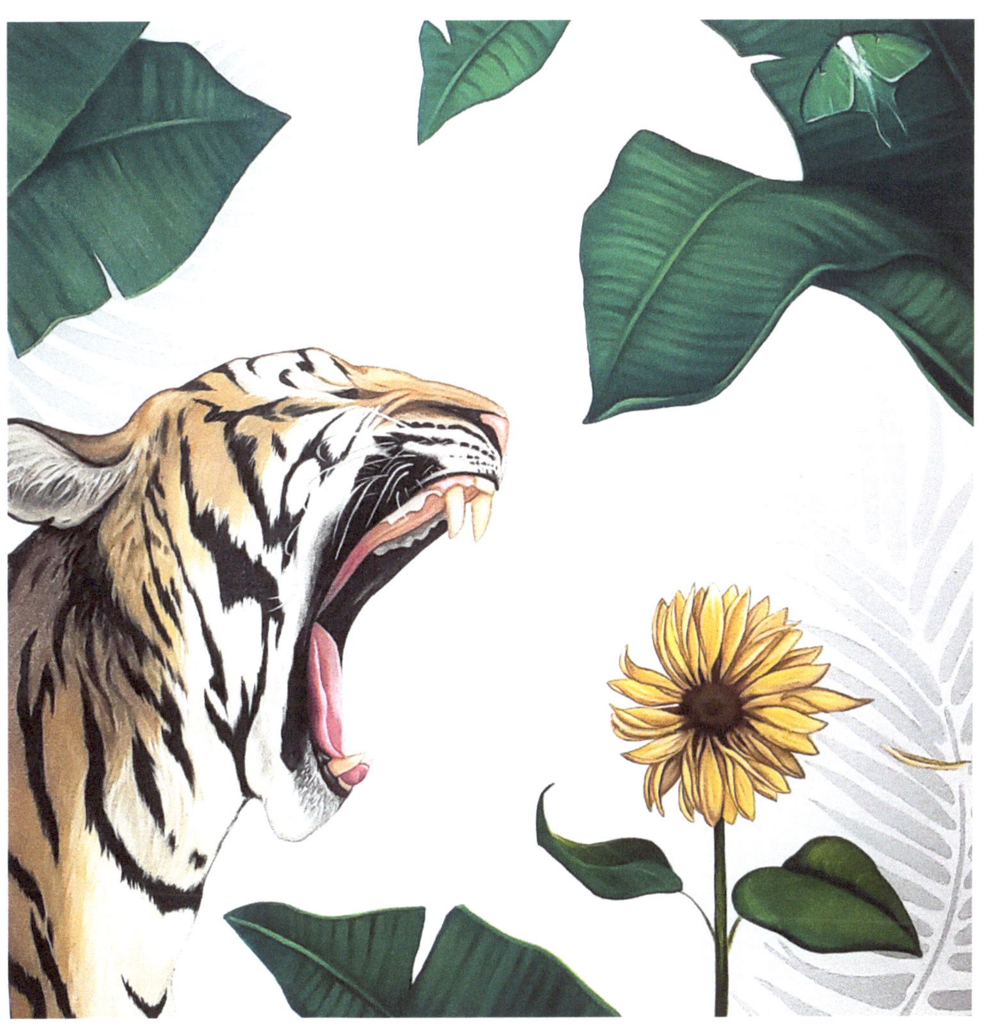

Tiger's Gonna Tiger
24 x 24 in.
oil and acrylic on canvas

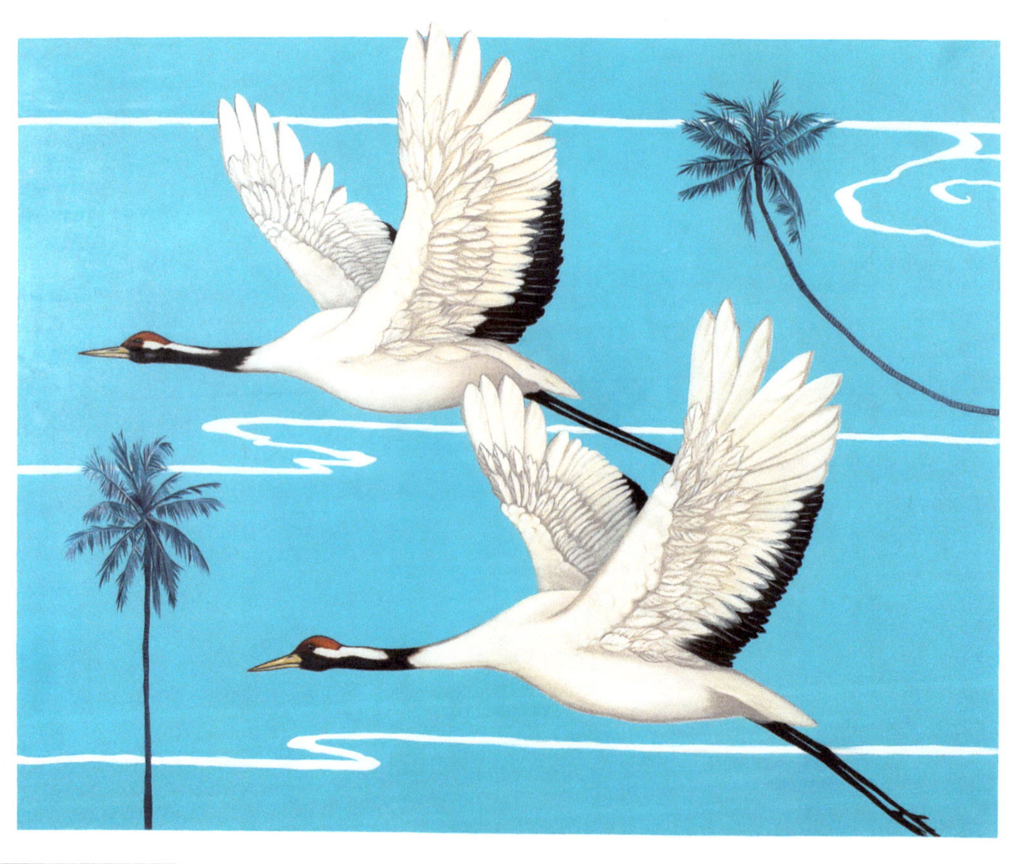

If You're Free, Free Someone Else
48 x 60 in.
oil and acrylic on canvas

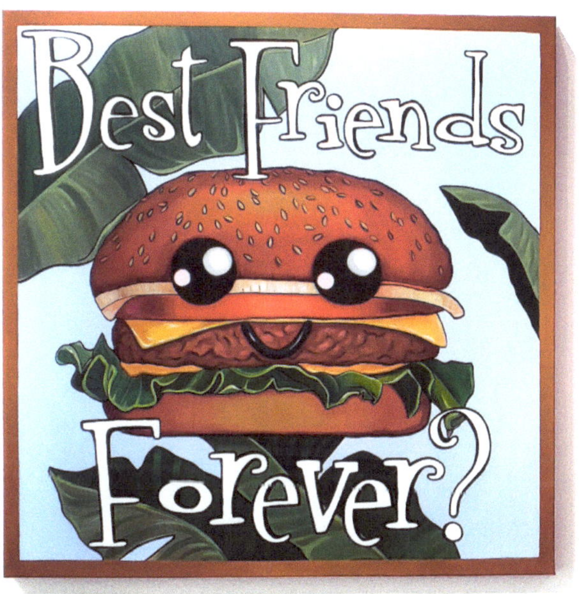

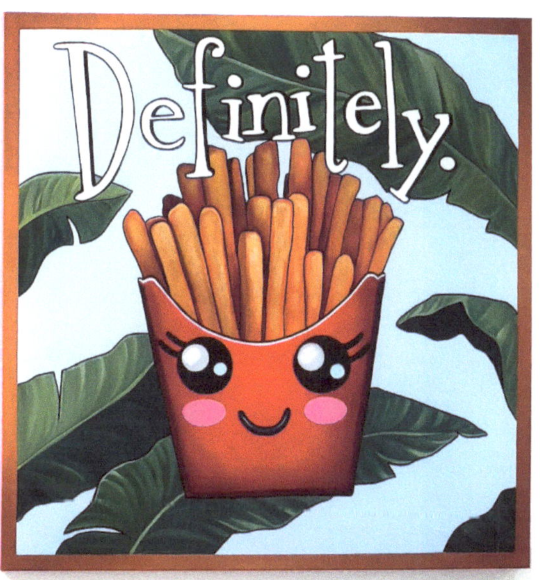

Burger + Fries Forever
48 x 96 in. diptych
acrylic and ink on canvas

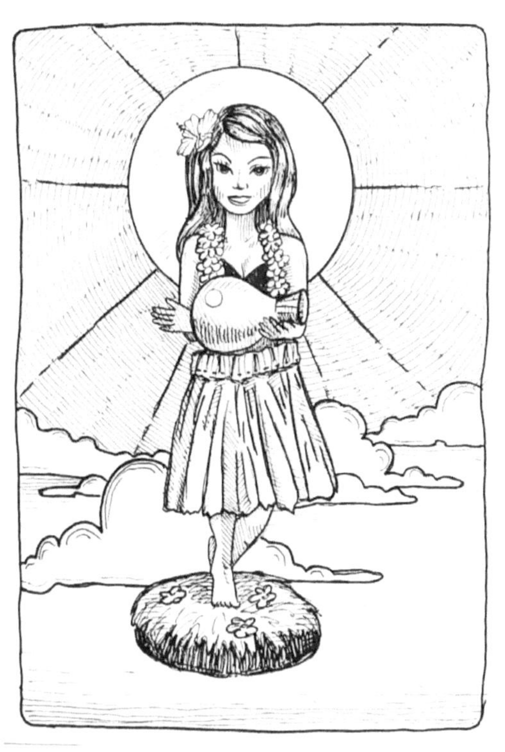

Ipu Hula
7 x 5 in.
ink on paper

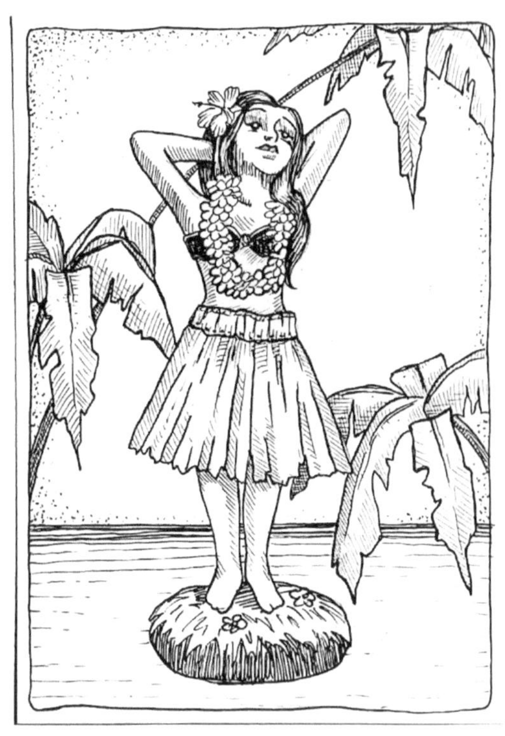

Happy Hula
7 x 5 in.
ink on paper

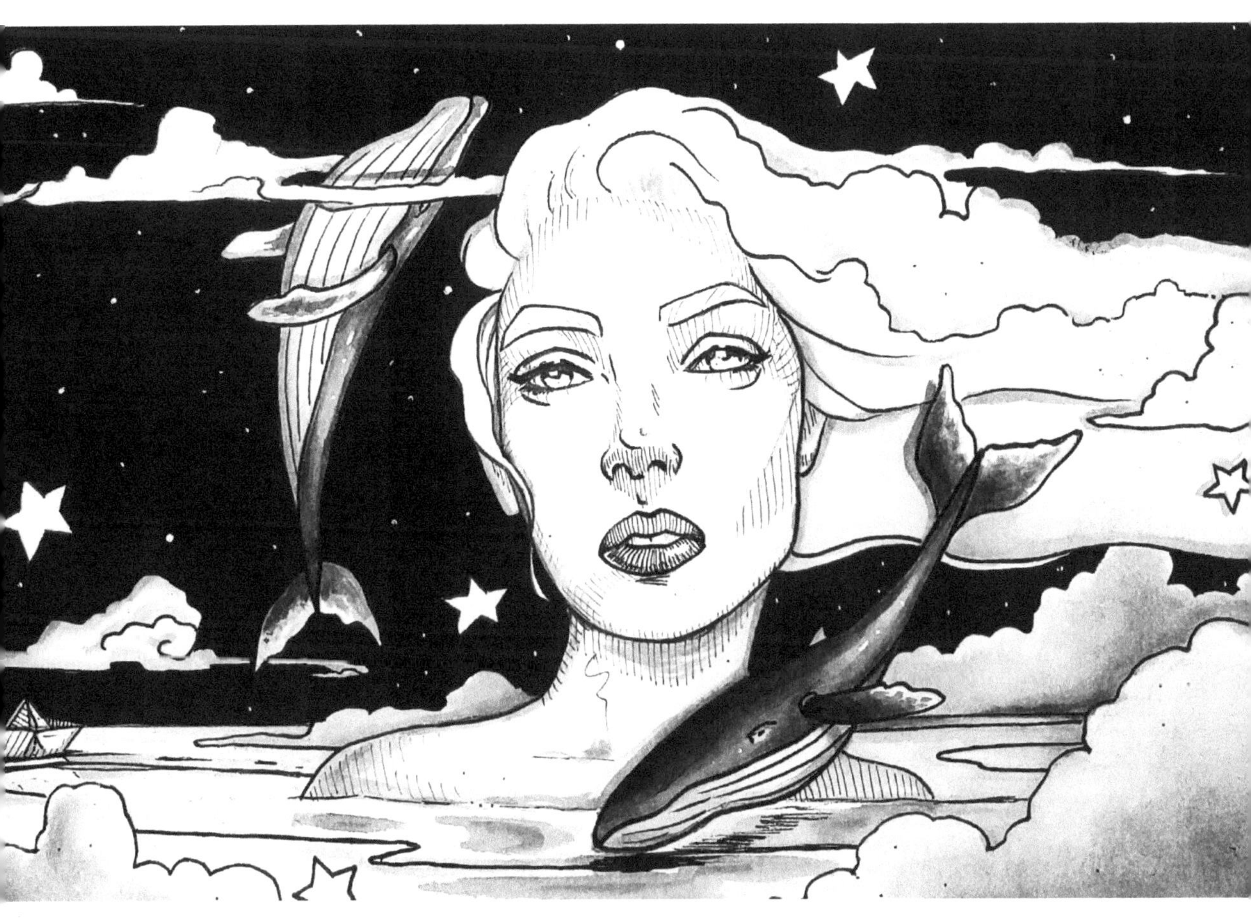

In A Dream
6 x 9 in.
ink on paper

two words
full of power
can change the world
if only they were used
two words

love

empathy

Photography: Asoggetti on Unsplash

There were no lights on in the home,
only a sad, lonely old man
hiding from the world on a Halloween night.

Photography: Alex Boyd on Unsplash

Descent into Marriage

Words:
Douglas King

Original Photography:
Frans Hulet
Unsplash

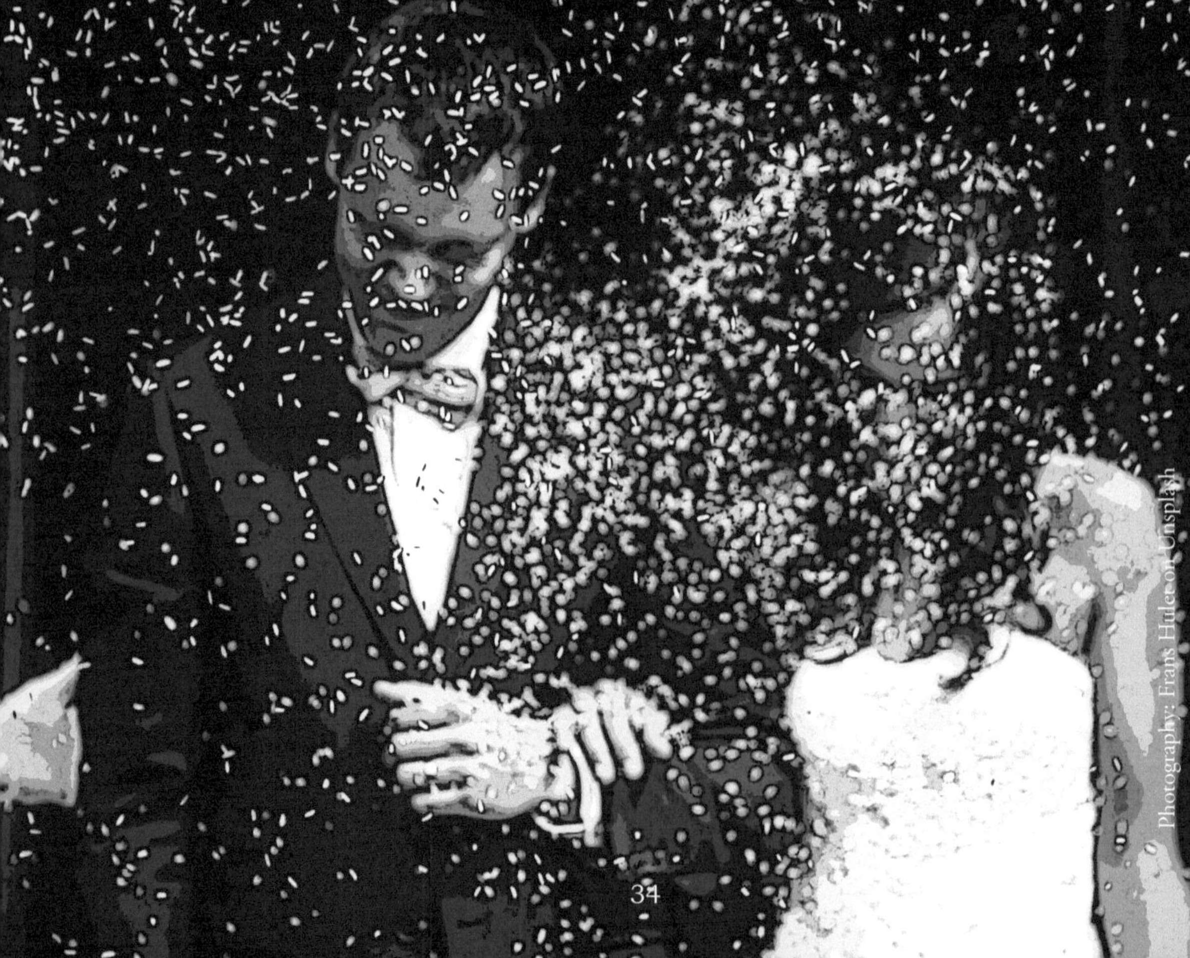

He went willingly.

Looking back, some would report that he even was excited and enthusiastic to take the plunge. The point is, he was not coerced in any way, shape, or form.

This is the story of one man's descent into marriage.

Upon meeting Haley Reed, Matt Dunklemann—the subject of our report—confessed to feeling the sensations of light-headedness, flutters in his stomach, and a general sense of giddiness, with a mild case of nervousness and trepidation. The two first met at a hipster coffee shop. (This is 2019 after all, and it would seem most serendipitous meetings—what screenwriters would call the meet-cute, which isn't even good grammar for writers to use—take place at a coffee shop because, of course, that is where people of the age who want to meet people hang out most often.) It should go without saying that the odds of two people meeting and falling in love at one of the houses of the roasted bean are extremely high, but we will go ahead and say it anyway.

After meeting and exchanging "digits"—the act of sharing one's telephone number—Dunklemann attempted to go back to his previous nonchalant existence but, as he has admitted, this proved futile. All he could do was think about Reed—about her hair, the color of her eyes and how they glistened in the single beam of sun that pierced the drawn shades of the window that late afternoon to alight, just perfectly, on her iris, which proved to be the most magnificent shade of blue, almost azure, like the waters of the most lovely South Pacific island.

He also spent copious amounts of time thinking about how soon he could call her without seeming desperate, but not wait too long and seem like he wasn't interested and was a "playa" (the term used for a man, or woman, who slept around with multiple partners). Dunklemann confessed to hating the "game" of dating, and it was the main reason he was not in a relationship at the time he met Reed. It was, in fact, a serious contributing factor in why he moved so quickly to propose marriage to Reed. He said it was an attempt to "avoid the madness of dating and just get on with it."

The time spent thinking about Reed instead of his work, self-care, other friends, or anything to do with world politics was the slippery slope that ultimately led Dunklemann to propose on that August day. It was Dunklemann's entire thought process after the event of meeting Reed that led us to conduct this research paper in the first place and which presented Dunklemann as the subject of further study into the madness that relationships cause on the human brain.

During the first interview with the subject, Dunklemann, we asked what he was thinking about at that exact moment. Instead of having any concern for his well-being, where he had been secretly transported, and why, in fact, he had been transported at all, with a hood over his head, to a secret black site, Dunklemann confessed that he was thinking about Reed. She was smiling at him while standing in a field made of rainbow-colored grass, with happy face clouds floating in the sky. He could smell the faint scent of lavender, which, it was soon deduced, was the scent of perfume that Reed was wearing the day they met. A thorough examination of Dunklemann was conducted, including a toxicology report, and it was determined that the subject was not on any form of hallucinogenic or other pharmaceuticals.

Released back into his natural habitat, Dunklemann proceeded to live out his life with one primary goal: to make Reed the happiest person on the planet, even to the detriment of his own happiness and well-being. Many a man has succumbed to this madness and, again, it is for this reason that Dunklemann was selected as a test subject, especially because of the extreme severity of his condition.

The term "love is blind" was coined in 1953 by the famed scientist Dr. Reginald P. Maynard while studying the subject Harold Flotsmyer, who literally plucked his own eyes out of his head so that he would never look upon another woman after he fell in love with Pattie-Anne Hogsmith of Topeka, Kansas. This was the first study of the maddening effects of relationships on a man's brain.

Extensive research continued for the next two decades. Even DARPA conduct a test in the early 1970s to see if they could weaponize emotions after witnessing the effects of "free love" on a generation of "long-haired hippie weirdos," a direct quote from General George Easterland III, a fourth-generation military man who could not, for the life of him, understand what "all the nonsense is." After failing to produce an actionable weapon, General Easterland wrote in his final report: "I married to procreate and that is all. Emotion does not need to play a part in a man's life as long as he can spread his seed to continue his name and has the ability to defend himself against any enemy like those damn commies."

But we digress.

We remained vigilant in studying Dunklemann for the five months, 14 days, six hours and 28 minutes it took him to get down on one knee in front of Reed and propose marriage while visiting the very same beanery they first met in, and only after having placed their order for the very same Americano, for him, and a double-shot iced caramel macchiato with a hint of vanilla, for her. The entire coffee shop was enraptured waiting for her response. Witnesses later said it felt like an eternity before Reed responded with an affirmative in acceptance of his proposal. (One could easily argue that for some living in alternate realities or in a temporal plane outside of a black hole or other quantum field, where time shifts and bends like the very fluid in a coffee mug, it did take an eternity. But that is not the purpose of this report.)

Needless to say (yet we will say it anyway), the entire java joint went off in celebration, like Boston after winning the World Series in 2013. Thankfully, no one was hurt, and the one apparently homeless gentleman, who did attempt to flip a table, was stopped before he could complete the maneuver. The couple received their drinks on the house as a token of gratitude for allowing the mocha mansion to be part of their formative years.

It was suspected that the madness would subside in Dunklemann after proposing and, in fact, be transferred to Reed, who immediately called her mother, all of her friends, and even two women she was not friends with but wanted to, pointedly, let know that she was engaged and would be married long before "their worn-out asses ever would be." In truth, the madness in both subjects only increased.

It was natural, in the mind of this researcher, that Reed's madness would increase, because the act of preparing for a wedding has been statistically proven to induce mania, no matter how "controlled" and "realistic" a future bride says she will be in planning the day of her nuptials. What was, in fact, surprising for this researcher is just how much further the madness deepened for Dunklemann during this time. The man was involved—happily, we might add—in every decision that needed to be made for the big day. Not only did he attend every cake tasting, food tasting, and invitation addressing event, he actually, and we are not making this part of the report up, was proactive in determining the exact paper weight and color of the invitations, and he was instrumental in selecting the color, quantity, and quality of flowers, not only for the table centerpieces, but for the bride's own bouquet as well.

It was at this point, based on all we had seen in first-person accounts and heard in extensive interviews with friends, family, and the main subjects, that we concluded that Mr. Matt Dunklemann was, in fact, truly, completely, head-over-heels, red-level, stage-four, madly in love.

The effects of which are often confused with a psychotic split with reality.

End of report.

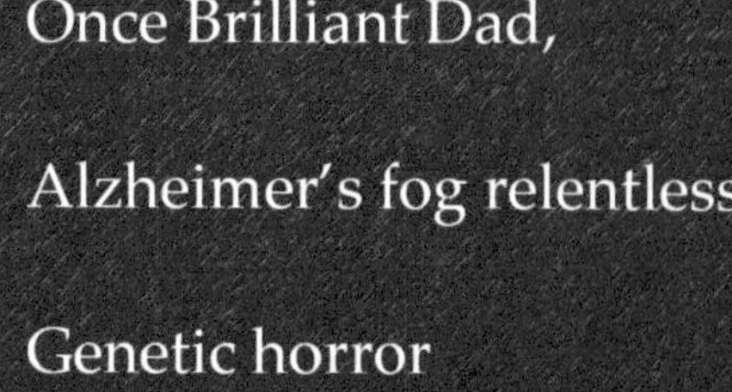

Once Brilliant Dad,

Alzheimer's fog relentless

Genetic horror

Photography: JD Mason on Unsplash

My soul is crushed
under the reality
  of the jest;
by the weight
  of indifference;
by the force
  of unrequited emotion.

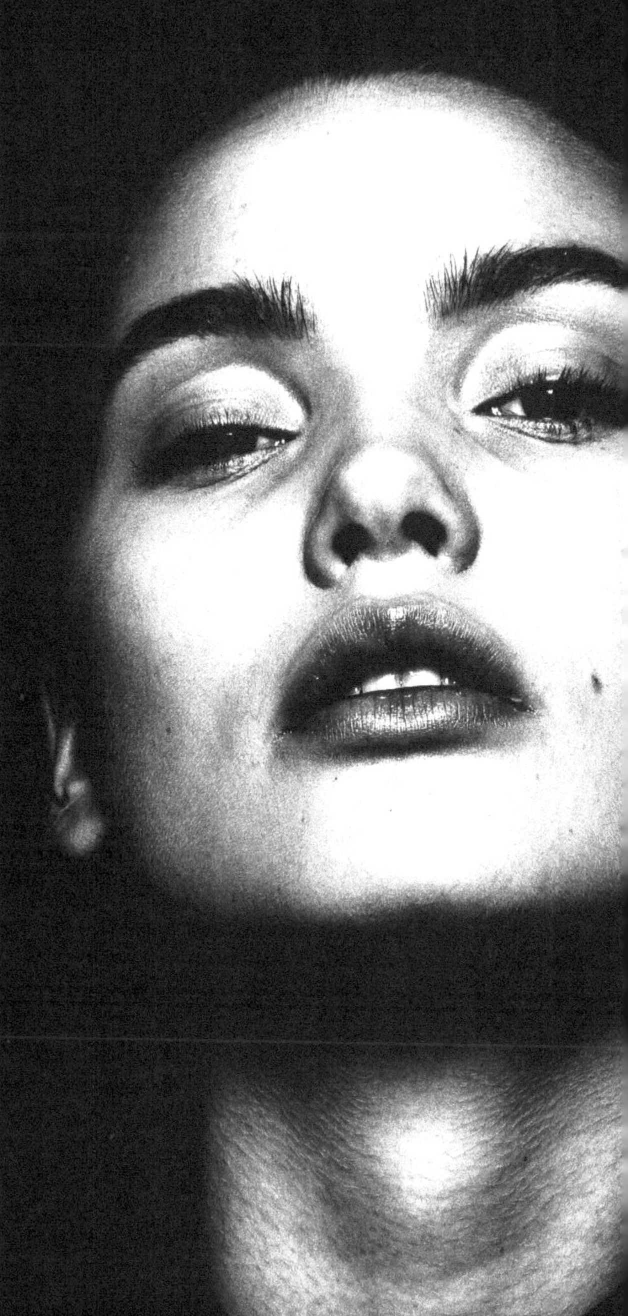

Photography: Peter Sjo on Unsplash

I am haunted by the question

why?

and there is never an answer

Photography: Dasha Yukhymyuk on Unsplash

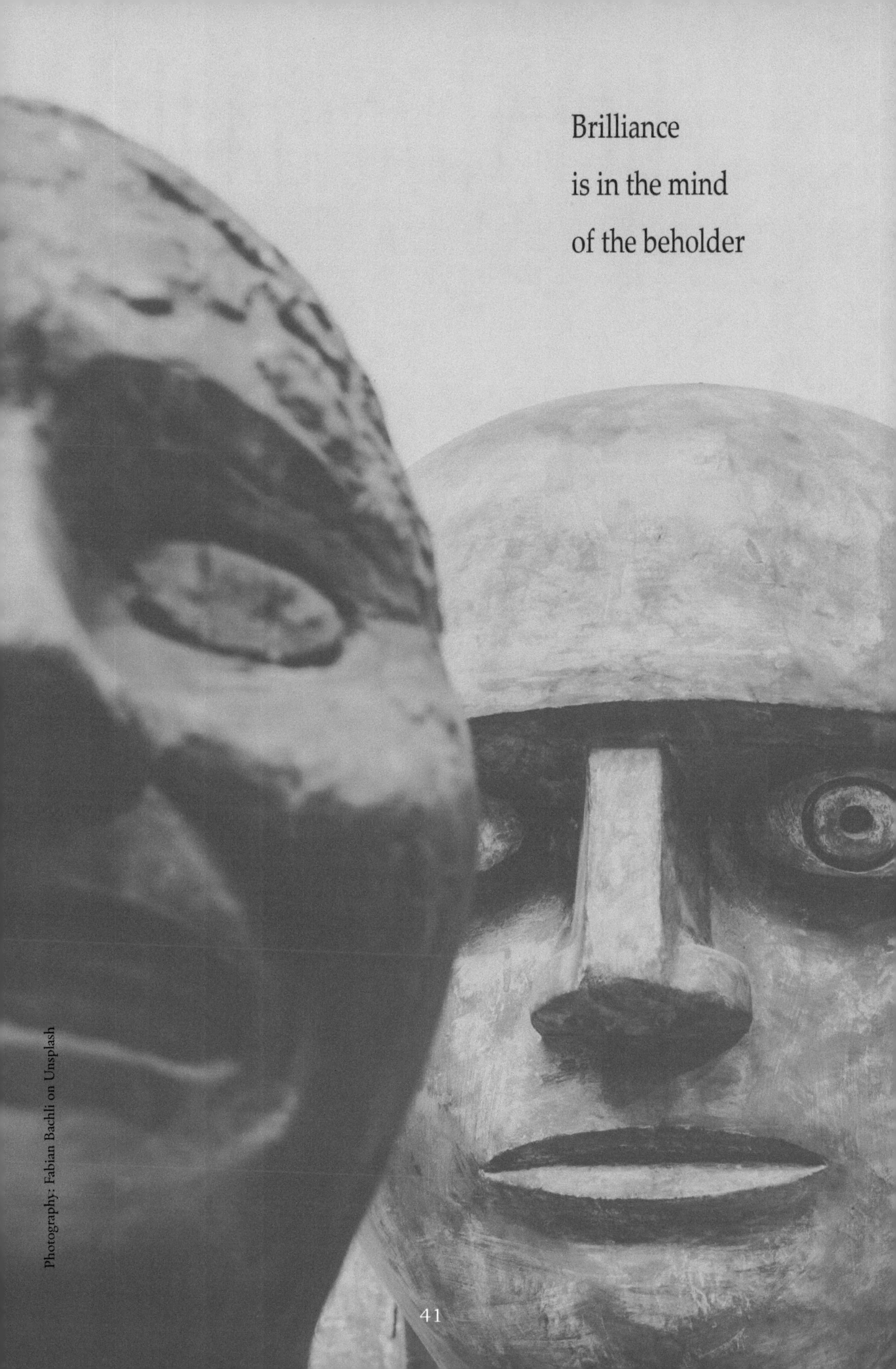

Photography: Fabian Bachli on Unsplash

Orientation Day

Words:
Douglas King

Original Photography:
Luis Villasmil
Unsplash

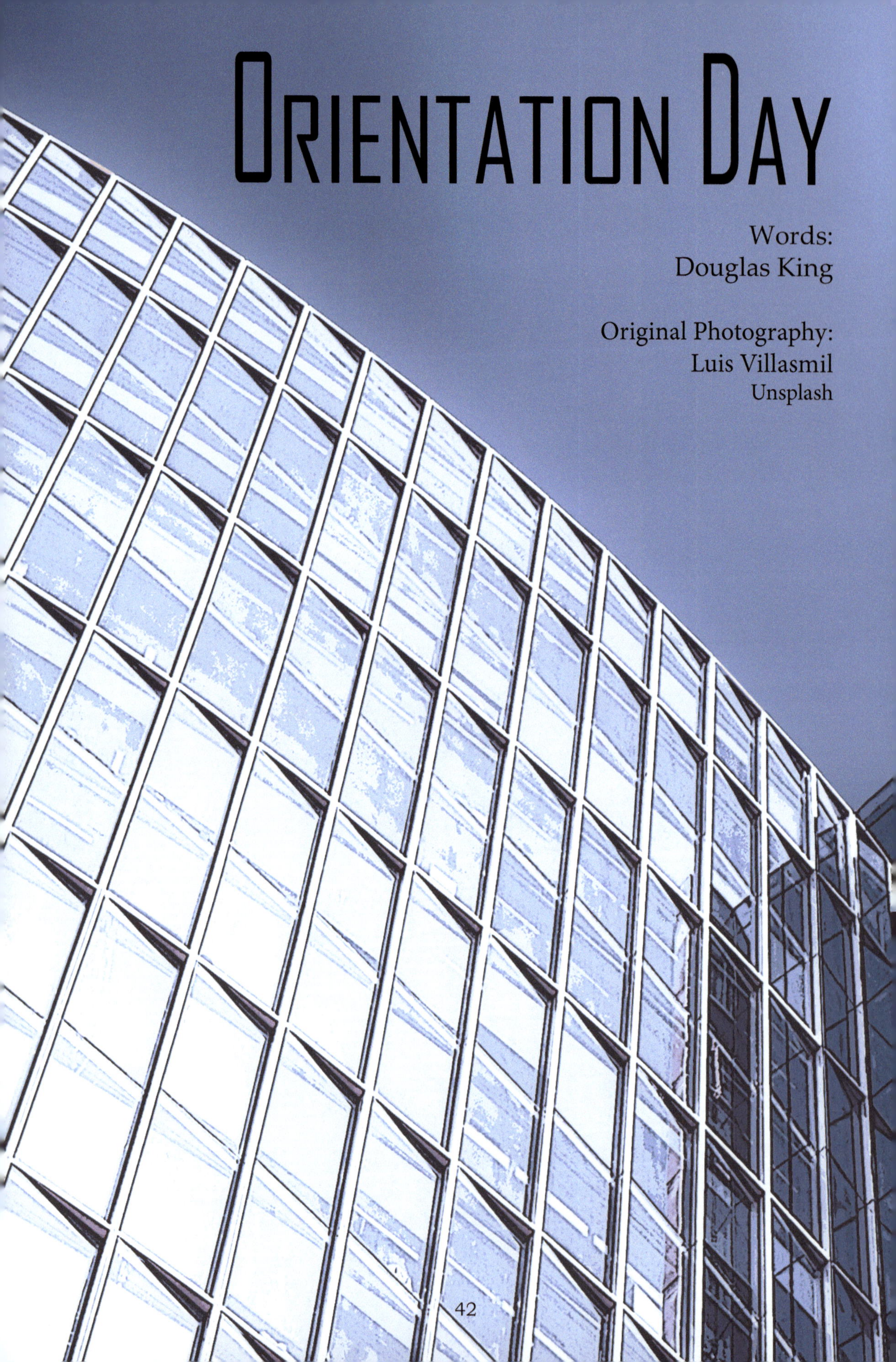

"Watch your step."

The human resources representative pointed to the clearly defined—by brilliant yellow paint—edge of the stair, as she continued the tour of the Mytel Data campus.

Mytel was one of the leading crypto-data companies, with revenue greater than some developing nations, whose services were used by nearly half the population of the planet, including those who lived in said third-world countries. Thanks to a 3,600 percent increase in valuation since its launch in 2020, the company had increased its staff to over 27,000 employees—27,342 to be exact.

It was employee 27,342 who was being given a personal tour of the supersized campus, also known as the Mytel Community.

Today was employee 27,342's first day. Orientation day.

"First stop will be the rec center. We offer an activity for nearly every interest. I'm not joking," the HR rep said with a smile on her face. "We, of course, offer rock climbing, yoga, meditation rooms, basketball, racquetball, volleyball—nearly all the ball sports—but we also have the only campus with a professional wave pool for surfing, as well as a white-water river for paddle sports. You may already know this, but our founder is a world-class water sport athlete."

"Yes, I read his memoir. He SUP'ed the Nāpali coast of Kaua'i by himself. That's extreme. I did it with a tour," 27,342 said.

The HR rep smiled politely.

"These are the Commons; there are eight in total on the campus. Each is color coded, so you can reference them easily if you plan to meet friends. Each offers bike paths, community gardens, greenbelts, etc. It's basically a huge parklike setting, just for the company."

The HR rep led 27,342 along a path, under a canopy of flowering plants, and then out into the sun and what seemed like a greenspace nearly as large as Central Park.

"There is even an orchard in Green Commons. It's small, but it does provide apples, oranges, and grapes. Most of which are used by the various cafés around campus. All organic. All fresh. All the time."

27,342 could tell the rep had researched and repeated that line hundreds, if not thousands, of times. She must have been proud of herself for coming up with that pithy quote.

The two walked along the path. The rep waved to people she knew and continued chattering about all that the campus had to offer.

Soon, they came to a couple sitting on a park bench near the walkway. It looked like they were enjoying a family picnic with their young son. The HR rep stopped and introduced 27,342 to the family.

"This is Tom and Constance Lin, and their precious little boy. How's this little man?" The HR rep tickled and cooed at the toddler, who burped and giggled.

"Nice to meet you," Tom said and reached out a hand to shake 27,342's, while also making sure his son didn't topple off the bench, which he was precariously dancing on.

"Tom and Constance have been with the company … a few years now?" the rep asked with uncertainty.

"About six. He was born two years ago, so yeah, we both came on six years ago," Tom answered, looking to his wife for confirmation. She smiled and nodded agreement.

"That is so great. Well, can't doddle, so much to show."

"Sure is. Great to see you," Tom said to the rep.

"Constance, I'll call you, so we can plan a game night. Chris wants a rematch," the rep said as she turned to walk away.

27,342 followed the rep as she continued walking, leading them toward a three-story structure that looked organic—not a single straight line formed its exterior.

"The Lins are great people. My husband and I just adore them. Their son is one of the first company children. You are aware that any child born while you work and live on campus is considered company property? It is clearly stated in the company employee manual."

27,342 nodded.

"At first people balked, but when you consider all the company provides, it only makes sense. I mean, if you invent something while working for a company it's their IP, so why would a child be any different? You're not married as I remember."

"No. I have a friend, though."

"Are they applying here?"

"Not sure."

"You understand that once you become an employee of Mytel and move to the campus, all outside relationships are overseen by the company?"

"Yes."

"Obviously, family is allowed to visit with the proper visas, and you are allowed a set number of holidays where you can go off campus. A spouse is granted a temporary visa, which allows them to move here to integrate into the campus, but if they do not wish to apply at the end of their visa, then the company initiates divorce proceedings on behalf of the employee. It is all pretty simple and clear-cut. That is the benefit of the campus. Everything you could ever want or need is right here and provided for you. It's the perfect epicenter for work, life, and play."

"I'm excited to be here."

"So, if your friend wants to visit, just let me know and I'll take care of the required paperwork for you."

"Thanks."

"And you don't have any kids? No. You just completed university, that's right. Sorry. I've processed so many new hires this week that you are all becoming a blur to me." The rep laughed as she continued to close the gap on the rec center she was leading 27,342 toward.

"So how does that work, if an employee has a kid and then their contract isn't extended?"

The rep paused ever so slightly, as if the question was uncomfortable. "I won't say it hasn't happened," she said in a tone different from her usual tour guide timbre. "But we maintain a nearly 99 percent retention rate with employees. I mean, why would you ever want to leave this place?"

The rep turned and looked back at the Commons they had just walked through.

"But, in the event that such an occurrence should take place, the company offers adoption options for the parents. The company calculates the potential revenue the future employee could generate and then discounts the expense and education for the child. It's a sophisticated equation that's used. The result is a fee the parents can choose to pay to the company to adopt their child."

The two reached the organic building, and the rep opened the door for 27,342. "After you," she said, returning to her sweet, chirpy voice. "Isn't this place amazing?"

It was. The entrance was an impressive three-story atrium with balconies on each floor looking down. Banners with famous sports figures in action poses draped down from the ceiling. An OLED screen filled a space two stories tall by double that wide. Projected on it were promos for classes, upcoming events, announcements for pickup games, and the occasional advertisement for sports drinks, power bars, and athletic equipment.

The space was filled with dozens of people in various athletic outfits. Some were dressed in shorts and tank tops, and it appeared that a cycle class had just ended, as a group of sweaty men and women in colorful yoga pants, sports bras, and T-shirts flooded out of a room and across the wide expanse of the lobby.

"Let's get your member card, which is different from your employee card, so you can begin using the facilities today. Do you play any sports?"

"A little. I want to, but I've spent most of my time making sure my grades were good enough to work here."

The rep smiled. "Well, you will have plenty of time to learn now. The center is open 24/7 and 365 days a year. There is always something going on."

The rep led 27,342 to a bank of monitors where she scanned 27,342's employee card, then quickly filled in the required dialog boxes on the screen. Soon, a new card spat out and came down a chute on the front of the cabinet. The rep picked it up and handed it to 27,342.

"Don't lose this. It was easy to get but, for some reason, if you lose a card, it is a red-tape nightmare to replace. There is a lanyard in your welcome kit, which I recommend you use for all your employee cards. We'll get you another for dining and one for entertainment. I wish we could consolidate all of the info on one card, but they tell me it's important to keep each area separate."

"Probably due to the size of the data set. I imagine that each facility gathers an incredible amount of data on each and every user for that specific process, whether it is eating habits or recreational habits. The amount of data would be so large that it would be imperative to keep each in its own close system. I imagine there are terabytes of data just for the rec center—people's personal preferences, records of workouts, personal health info ..."

"And, that's why you're in engineering and I'm in HR."

The rep led 27,342 away from the bank of computers.

"Did you want to see some of the facilities?" The rep asked, but 27,342 could tell from her tone that she would really prefer not to have to.

"No, that's fine. I'm sure there is a lot more to see ... and I don't want to take your entire day."

"There is so much more to see! We haven't even scratched the surface. There is The Hub, where all your entertainment is, movies, concerts, galleries, the latest VR and AR experiences.

Did you know we have our own Void? It's the coolest thing. I swear some of the tech geeks … oh, no offense …"

27,342 just smiled.

"I swear they would spend their entire day in there, if we let them. We had to put a time limit on the experience, so people would still work," the rep said, laughing.

The two left the rec center and the rep guided 27,342 across the Commons again, toward a path that led between two squat buildings. She pointed to a lone structure in the middle of the Commons with a sizable crowd gathered by it.

"That is one of many food stands dotted around the campus. They make the best smoothies. I recommend the Pineapple Passion. You're not lactose intolerant, are you? Well, no matter. They offer lactose-free, gluten-free, all the free-type options.

"There are also two dozen sit-down restaurants, a few fast-food chains, and a grocery store, of course, in case you like to cook. All food and dining is deducted from your salary based on use at the end of a pay period. You never have to worry about paying a bill again. So efficient and convenient."

The rep smiled her patented pleasant smile, which really projected no emotion whatsoever but was meant to give the impression that it did.

"If you like, you can download a complete accounting of your monthly expenses in the event you have a dispute with the deductions, but, honestly, I have yet to see the system make one mistake."

The rep flashed her smile again and continued walking.

"We'll check out The Hub next. You'll love it."

27,342 wasn't sure if the rep meant the comment because she perceived 27,342 was a tech geek or simply as a statement that The Hub was a very exciting, state-of-the-art entertainment complex. 27,342 had read about The Hub online before applying to work for Mytel. It was, in fact, one of the reasons 27,342 wanted to work there, but that would remain a private fact.

From the website, 27,342 knew The Hub was a personal directive of Mytel's founder, Nolan Collinshaw. Collinshaw founded Mytel after scoring a minor windfall when he sold his game app company. Collinshaw was a master at foreseeing trends and being ahead of the curve. The technology he created for crypto-data mining and protection was still the leader in the industry.

As Mytel grew, so did the staff required to stay ahead, and so Collinshaw set the standard for corporate campuses as well. The website stated that there were predecessors, but it gave Collinshaw the credit for defining the current age of corporate campuses and the laws that were put in place to enforce the new lifestyle required of those who worked and lived there.

27,342 was well versed in the history of Facebook's and Google's campuses, some of the first to be built. Facebook's campus had 21 buildings, 1,500 houses, office space, retail, and a hotel. While Facebook and Google may have been the first, and were often imitated by Microsoft, Amazon, Raytheon, Proctor & Gamble, and others, it was Collinshaw who not only hired the greatest architects and city planners, but who also lobbied the government to pass a bill essentially making it mandatory for full-time employees to work and live in the same place.

27,342 realized that the rep had been droning on with her chirpy boilerplate orientation, and they refocused their attention on what she was saying.

"… And if you like plays, we offer the latest touring Broadway shows. There are two galleries, a fine art collection—sponsored by our own Mr. Collinshaw—and a rotating exhibit of contemporary artists. At least once a quarter we allow an Unbounder to have residency while their exhibit is showing. They are completely vetted and cleared, don't worry," the rep added, before 27,342 could raise a concern, as if 27,342 would.

It was common practice for the many corporate campuses around the nation to allow Unbounders, those who were not permanent employees and residents of a campus, to receive temporary visas to stay on campus for a short time during a specific event, like an art exhibit or concert series. Unlike family members, who received a visa, the Unbounders were never recruited for permanent residency, mostly because it was a known fact that they would never consider moving to a campus. It was against some unwritten code of ethics and honor the Unbounders all shared.

Unbounders, more often than not artistic types of one form or another, were by their very nature more nomadic and free-spirited. When the laws changed and corporations forced employees to sign lifelong contracts, becoming "family members" of a company, many people refused the opportunity the corporations offered and preferred to fend for themselves outside of the protection of a company.

27,342's parents were this way, but they were older and accustomed to living in that manner. Most people born in 27,342's generation were now fully indoctrinated into the campus lifestyle. Gone were the days of worry about finding an affordable place to live, maintaining a working vehicle to transport one to and from work, and all of the other stresses that past generations had to deal with. Now, as the recruitment brochures—which every freshman student received when they entered university—promoted, the campuses offer not only a fantastic working environment, but a family-friendly environment where employees can live, eat, play, and enjoy all of the aspects of life without ever having to leave.

The societal benefits were profound as well, and that's why 27,342 could never understand why anyone would not want to live on campus. Among other things, commuter traffic disappeared. This resulted in a reduced level of smog and carbon emissions. The unemployment rate hit a record low and stayed there. Even those who were unqualified for tech jobs—those who had been employed in hourly-wage jobs—were able to become family members, taking jobs in food service, housekeeping, and other service-oriented tasks, just as before, but now with the comfort and safety of living and working in a closed community.

27,342 didn't personally know any Unbounders, but he had heard stories, and he hoped he never would meet one, other than the ones who were hired to create a well-rounded and balanced community on a campus. 27,342 knew those Unbounders wouldn't create trouble like the ones who protested and rioted when Collinshaw created his campus and had his law passed by Congress.

"… There is also a space for family members to display their art in juried showcases. Do you paint?"

27,342 quickly snapped out of deep thought. "No, I've never been much of an artistic type."

"Well, if you want to learn, there are classes for that, too."

27,342 wondered if the rep stayed this perky all the time. It seemed like she was a ball of sunshine walking on thin little human legs. It must be exhausting to be around her all the time, 27,342 thought and wondered what her home life was like.

"We have some amazingly talented family members," she said as they continued walking.

They circled a roundabout walkway after passing between two buildings into another Common area. Like the weenies that Walt Disney incorporated into every theme park, the

Frank Gehry-designed Hub revealed itself in all of its splendor and magnificence. 27,342 recognized the building from the photos online.

"Mr. Collinshaw worked closely with architect Frank Gehry on the exterior form of the building. It's meant to represent man reaching for infinity," the rep explained.

27,342 could clearly perceive the two outstretched wings of the building reaching skyward on either side of a spherical core, which 27,342 knew housed a state-of-the-art planetarium and an IMAX Dome screen. On approach from this perspective, the building did in fact look like an impressionistic figure gazing heavenward.

Inside was even more impressive, and 27,342 tried not to gawk in complete admiration and excitement.

The multistory building was on par with any Las Vegas casino. The interior was a multisensory experience orchestrated and balanced so as to provide optimal excitement and information while not overwhelming or confusing the viewer. Music, video, lights, and even smells, were all perfectly engineered in a syncopated dance of media seduction. Projections of the latest film trailers played while music blared from kiosks leased to entertainment companies such as Apple, Netflix, Amazon, and more. The Hub was an entertainment lover's wet dream.

As 27,342 scanned the kiosks and queues for various entertainment venues, the thought occurred that inside this building, on this campus, was the work of people who worked and lived on other campuses, much like Mytel's—though not as good, if you believed the marketing. 27,342 wondered what life was like on those campuses and knew they had to use Mytel's technology (everyone did), so the campuses were in fact, much like symbiotic organisms that helped the others exist on some level.

It was a comforting thought for 27,342 to know that life was arranged now and that there would be little stress in taking care of the basic necessities, like 27,342's parents had had to deal with. With the passing of the employment laws, people were no longer transient with their careers—changing jobs every year or so—and the worry of finding a place to live that was cost effective and close to work was completely eradicated.

27,342 only realized the rep had stepped away when she returned, smiling, and placed another card in 27,342's hand.

"This will give you access to everything in The Hub, deducted from your salary, naturally. Some items are complimentary, and often we hold company-wide events where special concerts or film premieres are hosted by Mr. Collinshaw."

27,342 accepted the card and clipped it to the lanyard, along with the employee and rec center cards.

"I hope you didn't mind me leaving you for a moment. I could tell you were a bit hypnotized by everything, and I thought I would allow you to enjoy it all a bit longer," the rep said.

"Sorry. I've seen the pictures online, but they pale compared to the real thing."

The rep spun and took in the sights and said, "Yes. It really is amazing and needs to be experienced in person."

There was only the briefest of pauses before the rep started up again. "If you've seen enough, I can show you your living space. You will want to get settled in and rest."

If left alone, 27,342 could spend an entire day lost in thought. And, in fact, actually had.

"I could spend all day here," 27,342 said.

"Well, don't do that, silly, I'd have to put your first demerit in your file," the rep replied, trying to be funny.

"Oh, I won't," 27,342 said, trying to recover.

The rep smiled and turned to leave.

27,342 lingered a little longer, taking all of the spectacle in.

"There is a complete guide for all showtimes and events on the MyChannel, which you can access via the app or the TV in your condo. It's easier just to download the app on your phone or watch," the rep said, pointing to the smartwatch on her wrist.

"Yeah, I downloaded the app before orientation this morning."

"Look at you being all proactive. This way."

27,342 followed as they walked back out into the Commons area and turned right. The rep consulted her tablet computer.

"So … It looks like you're housed in the new Porter Hall, named after Mr. Collinshaw's son, Porter. He was born on August 16 at 5:47 PM. An 8-pound, 4-ounce laughing baby. Have you seen the baby photos online? Oh. My. God. He is the cutest bundle of joy I have ever seen."

27,342 had seen the photos. They were hard to miss; the birth of Porter was a highlight not only for any future family members of Mytel, but for much of the world, considering the prominence of the baby's father. Porter's birth was equal in prestige to that of the royal family.

"Let's grab a tram to Porter Hall, since it is quite a walk. The tram stops are clearly labeled by the red circles with blue horizontal lines. Mr. Collinshaw is a huge fan of the London Underground. So, the graphics team decided to pay homage to the public transit system by replicating the logos and graphics. Each stop has a name, and there is a map at the stop telling you which lines to take. You can also access this info by, yep, you guess it, the app. Mytel's transportation system is one of the most state-of-the-art in the world. Not only do we have driverless trams—and have never once had an accident of any kind—but there is a monorail system based on Disneyland's. Another of Mr. Collinshaw's loves. He is a student of all things Disney."

The HR rep was like a Wikipedia on Collinshaw and Mytel information, and as she spoke, it was like listening to the PR department.

"The monorail is good for longer trips across campus and if you are really in a hurry. The trams are efficient and always on time, but there are a lot of stops, so plan ahead."

27,342 followed as the rep led them to a tent-like structure, which, sure enough, had the classic red circle bisected by a blue horizontal bar, with the words "Purple Common." The rep pressed a color-coded button to call the tram.

"The trams run like clockwork, but I always recommend pressing the call button anyway. On slow days, the trams park to conserve energy. Everything runs as efficiently as possible."

The two stood in silence for the first time since they left the HR department. It was a short silence.

"You're going to love Porter Hall. I wish I could move there. They just completed it a month ago, I think. Now, I'm not sure you are aware, but our living spaces do not have many amenities since the campus offers you everything you need."

"Sure."

"Not many people know, it was those amenities that partly caused the rise of the corporate campuses. It's true. The cost of apartment living became so high that no one could afford to live anywhere. I'm not talking about marble tile and granite counters. It was the libraries, movie theaters, gyms, pools, yadda, yadda, yadda. Did you know that in San Francisco, if you made $170,000 and lived in the city, you were eligible for housing assistance? How crazy is that? That's when Mr. Collinshaw decided things had to change. That and the cost of insurance and maintaining transportation. It just got to be too much. Thankfully, Mr. Collinshaw had a vision. Oh, here's our ride."

The rep stopped talking long enough to remove her employee card from her pocket. 27,342 noticed a colored lanyard, which had been bedazzled by the rep to make it customized to her tastes.

"You'll need your employee card to ride any transportation. There is a minor fee to cover maintenance—really minor—which will be drawn directly from your salary."

The autonomous tram stopped with a few warning beeps and the door slid open. It was empty. The tram lowered to make entry easier and the rep stepped aboard, waving her card at a sensor box near the front door. 27,342 followed and mimicked the rep.

As it was empty, they had their choice of seats. There were seats along each side under the windows for about a dozen people to sit comfortably, and metal handholds allowed for another six to stand in the aisle. The rep sat near the front and motioned for 27,342 to sit across the aisle from her, giving them each a bit of private space.

"I doubt we'll encounter much traffic at this time of day, but one never knows," the rep said as chirpy as ever. "When the traffic is light like this, sometimes the trams will go directly to your stop if you program that into your app. Again, it's all about efficiency."

Pneumatic pumps filled with air and lifted the tram 6 to 8 inches, for a more appropriate cruise elevation, and the door slid shut with a whisper. 27,342 heard the warning signal as the tram prepared to pull away from the stop and a few people hustled out of the way, but 27,342 knew that sensors set above the windshield would never allow the vehicle to move forward as long as it registered the presence of any kind of obstacle.

In fact, 27,342 was aware that the technology of autonomous vehicles had improved so much in the last decade that they were now 100 percent safer and a more efficient means of travel than old-style automobiles. Yet another reason that campus lifestyle was preferred—there was no need to own and maintain a vehicle. 27,342 didn't even have a driver's license or know anyone the same age who did. 27,342 was so impressed by the technology in autonomous vehicles, the thought of working for Kiva, the company that manufactured them, instead of Mytel, had been a dilemma for weeks.

Once the area in front of the tram was clear, it departed and quietly drove along the path marked with what 27,342 recognized were painted lines coated with an infrared paint. The sensors of the tram could detect the paint and then compute the border of where it could travel. 27,342 was fascinated by the tram and excited to be riding in it for the first time.

"We should be to Porter Hall in just a few minutes. If you don't mind, I need to check a few emails."

27,342 didn't mind and smiled, nodding. To be honest, 27,342 was happy at the reprieve from the rep's constant talking. Yes, the rep was friendly and accommodating, but 27,342 was used to long hours alone, studying, reading, or thinking. The few minutes of quiet during the drive provided 27,342 time to finally enjoy the idea of working for Mytel and living on this extraordinary campus.

The drive was too short for 27,342, but it did provide a few fantastic sights along the way. First was a tunnel filled with neon and colored LEDs in a hypnotic and almost psychedelic show. The tunnel was for trams only and allowed them to cruise at higher speed without the worry of any interference from humans. This also allowed for more greenspace on the surface.

Once they exited the tunnel, there was an array of high-rise superstructures that were the various living halls. Each had its own style and personality, giving the living quarters of the campus a cosmopolitan look and feel. The tram passed over a shallow canal where 27,342 witnessed people paddleboarding or riding leisurely on piloted gondolas.

Each hall had been designed by hand-selected architects. The list of predominate architectural firms was like a who's who of the world's greatest firms: Zaha Hadid Architects, Foster + Partners, Studio Gang, Adrian Smith + Gordon Gill Architecture, Kohn Pedersen Fox, and Büro Ole Scheeren, to name just a few. In all there were 50 towers, each offering 200-plus condos, spread across the campus. Porter Hall was one of a group of ten new towers that had been built in the last few years to accompany the growth of the company.

When 27,342 signed the employee agreement, there was a choice between high-rise living or private housing, where an additional 1,700 homes were situated around a lake setting. But those homes were mostly reserved for families.

The warning beep signaled that the ride was coming to its conclusion, and the rep completed her email and shut down the app on her tablet.

"Okay, we're here. Home sweet home." The sweet, chirpy tone was still present, even after all of the talking.

27,342 had never expected to live in a place so nice. The lobby looked like something in a five-star hotel, and the lift zipped them smoothly and speedily to the 25th floor. The smell of fresh paint and new carpet filled the hall as the rep and 27,342 exited the lift.

"It still has the new car smell to it," the rep said, dating herself, with a phrase that hadn't had meaning for at least a decade. It was the first time that 27,342 noticed that the rep was actually closer to 27,342's parents' age. She must have had some work done, 27,342 thought. She certainly had aged well if not, and her demeanor was that of someone half her age.

The rep guided 27,342 down the hall and stopped before a door. She smiled and motioned toward it.

"After you. You should be the first to walk through the door to your new home!"

27,342 fumbled for the key fob, which was in the orientation packet. The black plastic electronic key was no bigger than a thumb drive, and 27,342 waved it over the circular sensor near the handle to activate the lock. A soft whir and a click let 27,342 know the key worked and door was unlocked.

Upon entering the condo, the first thing that was inescapable was the view. 27,342's condo overlooked the Commons they had just driven through, but from this lofty perspective the perception of the space was entirely changed. The paths that seemed so wide were small grey lines partially hidden by the mature trees. Green was the predominate color, followed by a streak of blue, which 27,342 recognized as the canal they had passed over. The ring of the other living halls, each named in tribute to a Collinshaw family member or a senior executive of Mytel, created the horizon line for the view, and 27,342 knew living here would be the best.

"As I mentioned, the television offers closed-circuit channels, so you can view the day's events and activities, schedule food deliver, order tickets, sign up for classes, and even watch lectures from tech leads from around the campus, in the event you can't get a ticket or miss the event. I believe each lecture is available for 72 hours after the live presentation. After that you have to use on-demand. You can also use the Mytel video conferencing system to chat with friends on campus and even connect with family off campus. They should have received a Telcom module, which they attach to their television so you can communicate."

"Yes, I helped install it."

"Wonderful. Let's see ... what else? Your bags should have already been transported and placed in your room."

The rep peeked into the bedroom, which was just off the entrance hall before reaching the living room.

"Yep, I see them there. There is a 24-hour concierge, if you need it, but with the MyChannel and the app on your phone, everything is really at your fingertips. Should any maintenance issue with the condo arise, then just ring down to concierge and they will take care of it."

The rep looked around the condo, which was pleasantly furnished with generic case goods and a sofa.

"You can replace any of the furniture. Mytel provides these furnishings when you first move in for convenience. It's easier than having Unbounder movers on property. It's all about efficiency and convenience. Just go on MyChannel and select condo furnishings, and you can choose style, color, whatever your heart desires. Let your fêng shui-flag fly," the rep said in an ill-attempt at a joke.

"Oh, and the most important thing!"

The rep stepped into the kitchen, which was off of the entry hall and open to the living room. She opened the refrigerator and a pantry.

"Stocked with some basics to keep you alive for a day or two, until you get to the store …" she said, laughing. "I totally forgot to take you by the mall."

"That's okay."

"I can't believe I did that. Especially considering I spend half my time there, it feels like." Another short laugh, kind of like the bark of a hyena. "I'm kidding. Well, sort of. I do like to shop. Oh, I must be tired, I'm starting to ramble. It has been a long week." She paused, collecting her thoughts. "If you want, I can take you over …"

"That won't be necessary. Really."

"You sure?" the rep asked, but 27,342 could tell by her tone and the look on her face that she was relieved.

"It's fine."

"Good. Well, if you need anything, don't hesitate to call me. You have my number?"

27,342 nodded.

"You can order groceries on MyChannel and they will be delivered right to your door. You can also order takeout. We have the best Thai food. Oh, and sushi! Italian. Stop, you're getting me hungry! Anyway, it's all accessible on your app."

The rep closed the door to the refrigerator, looked around, smiled, and said, "Well, that concludes your campus orientation. Tomorrow you will report to work orientation at 9 AM. You know which quad you're working in?"

27,342 nodded.

"Great. Do you have any questions for me? If not, I'll let you unpack and unwind. This is exciting! Welcome to the Mytel family!"

"I think I have everything I need, and I have a good idea where to find it if I don't." 27,342 pointed at the television.

"Oh." The rep laughed, realizing that 27,342 had been listening. "Okay, then. I'll leave you to it."

The rep smiled again and then exited. Finally, 27,342 was alone.

Returning to the window, 27,342 stared out at the view and realized that everything needed for life was easily and efficiently available.

Tiny little thought
don't run away
I would desperately like to hear
more of what you have to say
even though you are small
not more than an ounce you weigh
I would give anything for you
to sit and stay

Tell me, little thought
what makes you so gray?
did someone hurt you?
what keeps your joy away?
I'd love for you to experience peace
if only for a day
then, maybe you will feel
as I do, and we can finally play

Photography: Zdenek Machacek on Unsplash

My life has become an inconvenience to me.

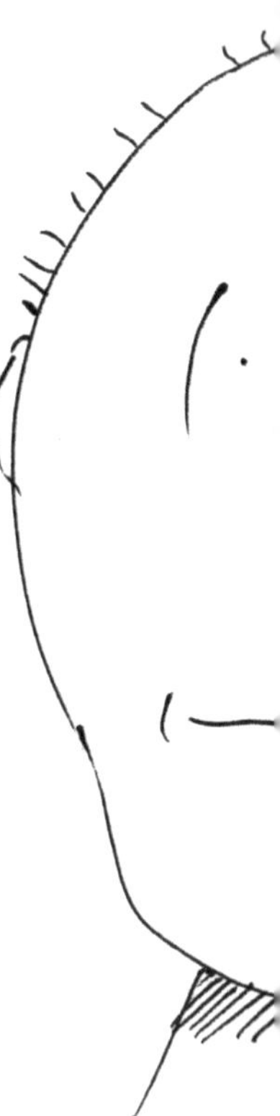

I wait for death

as one does a long-lost friend

I seek him out each day

yearning for his arrival

but he does not appear

just like happiness.

ET FINALE SERMO

Douglas King

Some are praised for being avant-garde, while others are chastised and berated for not following the rules. Who are these gods of taste and judgement to determine who should be exalted and who shall be stuffed down? Who are these tastemakers, these self-appointed dictators of art? How did they reach their position of judgement? How did they forget that they were pushed out of the same type of womb as the rest of us, and that we are all born equal—naked, cold, speechless, and with zero bowel control.

Is the taste of rarified air of the intelligentsia so powerful an aphrodisiac for fame and self-adulation that it renders the breather mummified from their past; do they forget who and what they were before achieving their status, thus transforming themselves into closed off and self-protecting hoarders of notoriety and wealth?

Are these just the ramblings of a jealous, envious hack who is bitter because he has not been accepted into this illustrious caste? Is it possible that these words are as meaningless as they are self-flagellating? That while the author thinks he is clever and witty, he is in fact just stringing words together in a nonsensical jumble of nothingness.

Or, could it be that he, like so many authors before him who string words together in a nonsensical jumble of nothingness, really spoke golden words of truth and sincerity, words that hold profound meaning?

This ultimately brings us back to the original statement: Some are praised for being avant-garde and radical, while others are berated.

Only time will tell which this is.

www.ingramcontent.com/pod-product-compliance
Lightning Source LLC
LaVergne TN
LVHW070220110826
845147LV00003B/612

* 9 7 8 1 7 3 5 0 0 8 3 0 1 *